Bridge to Redemption

CeCe Lively

ISBN 978-1-0980-3857-1 (paperback)
ISBN 978-1-0980-3858-8 (digital)

Christian Faith Publishing, Inc.
832 Park Avenue
Meadville, PA 16335
www.christianfaithpublishing.com

This book has Christian themes and the scenes are set in real-world scenarios. As you know, the real world isn't always nice. God's word tells us we are to be in the world but not of the world. Therefore, most believers have been exposed to profanity far worse than what you will read in this book. For character progression I have included some mild profanity, (hell and damn), these words are used sparingly throughout the book. There is also, what some may consider graphic, a scene of hell. If use of such words or Christian themes bother you, maybe this book is not for you. I understand your concerns and convictions. I hope that you will give my book a chance and read it with an open mind.

To my Lord and Savior Jesus Christ. Many years ago, he planted the seeds for this book and finally, my dream is fulfilled. Thank you, Lord, for the talent you have given me...at least I think I have talent. Thank you for pushing me forward through my self-doubt. I pray this book glorifies you.

To my husband Roger, without your support and encouragement this book would not have been possible. Your immense computer knowledge astounds and intimidates me! Without your expert help I would have lost the manuscript forever. I am blessed to have you as my friend and husband. I love you very much.

To Mollie, my partner in crime and fellow writer. Thank you for your assistance, and persistence in helping me finish this book. I applaud you for your patience, for listening to dialogue ideas both good and atrocious. Through it all you encouraged me. I am fortunate to have you as a friend.

To Jeanne Felfe my editor, thank you for your tireless efforts and your patience. Thank you for teaching me about Head Hops, and more about grammar than I'd ever care to know.

Chapter 1

Anxiety weighs down the heart,
but a kind word cheers it up. Proverbs 12:25 (NIV)

Being a Chicago cop was no longer a calling for Angus Connors. Tired of being shot at, harassed and heckled he started to doubt how much longer he could serve the citizens he swore to protect. Lately, he contemplated leaving the force. His belief that people were basically good was all but gone, and his tolerance for repeat offenders disappeared.

"Attention all vehicles. Domestic abuse in progress, 104 Park Boulevard. White female injured. Suspect is on scene. Agitated and intoxicated, wearing jeans and a white T-shirt." Angus nodded to his partner, and notified dispatch, they'd take the call.

"Damn, here we go again!" Angus spun the squad car in a U-turn, tires squealing, racing to the third domestic assault that week.

He maneuvered the car down the street lined with rundown brick apartment complexes. Vagrants in torn and dirty coats stood at the corner light. Drug dealers, their customers, and hookers all scurried away like an anthill being kicked when the squad car drove past. The Happy Times liquor store did not look like a happy place, with its grimy storefront and steel bars covering its windows. A rusted-out car at the corner thumped vulgar music so loudly the cruiser's windows rattled.

The city's noise and smells assaulted his senses and on bad days it almost nauseated him. His intuition kicked in and he surveyed the neighborhood in the vigilant way only a cop could, watchful for something that might go wrong.

His partner, Chris Hutchins, radioed dispatch, "Arrived at scene, 104 Park Boulevard."

A ramshackle house with broken windows faced the busy street. Trash bags and beer bottles clung to the chain-link fence surrounding the property. Angus side-stepped over a full diaper near the curb as the two of them carefully got out of the cruiser. They approached the house with caution. A haggard, scary skinny woman in jeans and a cutoff mid-drift shirt with a torn sleeve sat on the crumbling concrete steps. She held her stomach, crying as she wiped her bloody nose.

Angus turned to Chris and seeing a man inside near the large window gesticulating wildly, said quietly, "Let's get her away from him and see what's going on. Don't forget to turn on your body camera. I don't have a good feeling about this one."

"Hello, ma'am, I'm Officer Chris Hutchins, and this is Officer Angus Connors. We received a call about a possible domestic abuse."

She looked up and snarled, "I didn't call no one."

"Nevertheless, someone placed a call, your shirt is torn, and you're bleeding. May I have your name, date of birth, address and phone number? And can you tell us what happened?" Chris asked taking out a pen and notepad to record the events.

"My name's Valerie Stubbs. Why do you need all that stuff about me?"

"It's policy, ma'am."

"I live here with my boyfriend. I took him his dinner, and told him to turn the volume down, and he got mad. Said he hates fried bologna and chucked a plate at me and to bring him a beer instead. Next thing he's hitting me and pushing me into the wall."

"What's his full name? Does he have any priors?" He paused for a moment. "Is there anyone else in the house? Any children?"

Angus eyed the door. Valerie looked at him. Shaking and crying, she readjusted the bloody rag and wiped away her tears.

"Rick Woods. Been living together for 6 months. Do I gotta do this? I already told you, I didn't call no cops," she lied. Valerie bit her lip, knees bouncing as she spoke.

"Are there any witnesses? Any guns?"

"No, just me and him. No guns as far as I can tell. He's drunk, and on something. He's a mean drunk 'specially when doin' drugs."

Angus added, "Okay, uh Valerie, it's mandatory we take photos for all domestic abuse calls. It's the law. Hutchins, you can take pictures and I'll talk to Rick. Valerie, can you step over here?" He pointed to a barren area on the lawn as Chris took out his cell phone for photos.

"Do I have to? He didn't mean to hit me." Weeping she walked to the spot anyway.

"Yes, we have to take pictures, and like my partner said the state requires photos for abuse. Can you please turn your head?" Chris snapped a picture. "We'll have to take him in. Can you pull up your sleeve?"

"No, no, you can't," she wailed. "Please don't arrest him."

Angus watched Chris take the pictures and then looked through the window to see Rick stomping and growing angrier as he watched Valerie. Pacing and clenching his fists, he paused to throw another half-empty beer bottle against the TV, sending rivers of the yellow liquid dripping down it, and the wall.

"Hey, Hutchins, take her to the car now. I think we got a problem here."

"Sure," Chris said and dragged a reluctant Valerie to the squad car.

The hair on Angus' neck rose—he was certain there would be trouble. Turning, he saw a blur of motion to his right, and he tried to sidestep Rick. "What the—"

Rick bolted out of the house, and barreled into him, knocking him off the stoop and onto the crunchy and dried out lawn. It took a split second for Rick to slam into him, leaving no time for Angus to react and draw his weapon in defense.

Rick was tall and sinewy, and agile for a drunk. The two hit the ground with a hard thud and Angus groaned from the impact. They wrestled, rolling over each other. Angus grimaced when sticker burrs dug into his arm.

Rick bit Angus on his forearm drawing blood, and made a grab for his gun. Angus rolled away from his reach, sending them onto the gravel driveway.

Chris raced over to Angus and Rick.

From the corner of his eye, Angus saw Chris leave Valerie and bolt toward him and Rick. Chris took aim and Angus tried to roll the big man between himself and Chris so his partner could get a clear shot as Angus wrestled Rick to the ground.

Before his partner could fire, Valerie ran past him and lunged at Angus, kicking him while screaming, "I love you baby. I didn't call the cops!"

The three of them fought. Rick and Valerie shouted expletives at Angus as he tried to disengage Rick who attempted to gouge his eyes.

Chris holstered his firearm and grabbed Valerie as she kicked Angus in the ribs. "Stop resisting."

She landed in the dirt as Chris drew his gun again. He tapped his shoulder radio and requested backup. Valerie hurled herself at Chris, wrapping her legs around his waist, scratching and clawing at his face. Chris yelled when her nails drew blood, and he twisted and turned. He struggled to reach Angus who was losing ground with Rick.

Angus rolled over and thrust his back into Rick as the assailant reached from behind and tried to choke him. For a brief moment he broke free. He ignored the acrid taste of fear and remembered what his training instructor said, "Fight dirty if you have to."

He thought fast to neutralize the threat. He tried to protect his neck as Rick rolled over and locked his legs around Angus' midsection while putting him in a choke hold again. Angus tucked his chin to his chest and grabbed Rick's arms and pulled with all of his body weight. At the same time, he planted his feet on the ground and pushed backward. Their bodies flipped, giving Angus a momentary advantage. Adrenaline surged through him. Rick slammed his knee into Angus' crotch, sending him into a dizzying spin.

Angus managed to roll back on top as Rick shoved at him with drug-induced superhuman strength. He rammed the palm of his fist against Rick's nose, and blood spurted out; it didn't faze him.

They spiraled across the yard onto the sidewalk. Valerie catapulted across the yard and leapt on Chris. He could not discharge his weapon. Angus reached for Rick's throat. Rick broke his hold. In one swift move-ment, Angus head-butted him, gained the advantage, and cuffed him.

Chris fell to the ground. Angus winced at the sound his partner's knees made when they cracked from the impact of Valerie's weight. She scratched Chris' face with her nails and deadlocked her legs around his waist. Jerking and twisting his collar to choke him, Valerie hung on. Chris staggered to his feet.

With no time to catch his breath, Angus yanked Valerie from Chris, pushed her to the ground, and cuffed her.

Chris stood and said, "Rick Wilson you're under arrest for domestic abuse, resisting arrest and attempting to kill a police officer."

"Stop, you'll hurt him," Valerie screamed. "Stop, oh baby, I didn't call the cops. I love you."

She slumped onto the littered, prickly brown grass crying, and in between sobs glared at Angus. Chris read the Miranda rights to her, and placed her in the backup squad car that had screeched to a stop, moments earlier.

Angus bent over to steady himself, removing the grass, stickers, and rocks from his pants. He looked at his arm and saw teeth marks. In the struggle the bite went unnoticed. He reached into his pocket and got a handkerchief to wipe the blood off his arm and muttered, "Great, just great, now I have to go to the hospital and get tested."

Chris wiped dirt from his pants, and said, "Ah, man my shirt is torn. There's gonna be a ton of paperwork for this report."

Chris read Rick his rights, and placed him in the car. The suspect turned and screamed racial slurs at him. The drunk spit and sneered. "You just wait, you'll be sorry." He released a string of swear words that would make a prostitute blush.

"Sure, get in," Chris said covering Ricks head with his hand to prevent him from banging it against the car's door.

Angus looked at Rick. Everything within him compelled him to drag the lowlife out of the car, beat him, and leave him for dead. He pulled himself from the satisfaction of his daydream, shook his head, and remembered his training to say as little as possible and remain in control at all times. He walked towards the cruiser where Chris stood taking more notes.

"Connors, that was close," Chris said.

"That was too close for comfort. I'm getting tired of this."

"Once a cop always a cop," Chris commented.

"This is getting old." Angus got in the car and waited for Chris to finish his conversation with the other cops who assisted them. He thought about small town life. The intense life and death moments of being a beat cop wore on him. Scenes like this were becoming too common and he considered the relative ease of the life of a small-town cop.

The constant traffic noise ringing in his ears, the honking, the cursing, swarms of people in a hurry: to get to work, to leave work, and especially in a hurry at the crosswalks. Even the birds and insects buzzed about to get the next morsel of trash thrown on the ground; in a hurry before another creature could pluck up the trash and take away their food. Hurry was his name for city life.

Overcrowding, the endless jockeying for a position at the front of a line, every line, no trees, and the dismal gray of concrete everywhere drained him. The sky-high rent nearly matched the height of the buildings, the traffic, and the continual struggle to find a parking spot: these and a few other daily irritations caused him to reevaluate big-city living. His mind wandered back home to faces he trusted, to a slower way of life. And though he hated to admit it, back home to his family and his small-town roots.

He realized it was time to take Sheriff Rex up on the job he offered him a week ago. He picked up his phone and called his sister.

***

"Hey, Clara, this is Angus."

"Geez, I think I'd recognize my brother's voice. What's up?"

"I'll be moving back to Riverside, next month."

"What? Really?"

"Yah, I called Rex and he said he has an opening, and I have the job if I want it."

"Didn't Dad play football with him in high school?" She then added, "He always looks so mean."

"I know and he is mean, but he is judicious in his justice. Dad said they called him T. Rex in high school because of his aptitude for dishing out pain on the field. It's a great reputation to have as a sheriff."

"I thought you hated Riverside and small-town life here in West Virginia? I recall you said 'Riverside, I can't wait to get outta here. There's nothing to do here, just a bunch of gossips looking in on everyone else's business. This is nothing but a God-forsaken, podunk, two stop-light, too many goobers, too many watering holes town.' What happened, did you finally get tired of big city life and finally wise up?"

"Actually, I'm tired of looking around and seeing concrete and skyscrapers. I'm also tired of being shot at. Sooo, can you look at places for me? It'll take me about a month to tie things up here."

"Sure, I'd love to, um, but don't you want to stay at home and return to the 'Shrine of Angus'?"

He cleared his throat. "The what?"

"That's what Dad and I call your bedroom. Mom never turned it into the sewing and crafts room. She still has your trophies on your desk, ribbons, and medals all over the walls. Your life-size football cutout from the state championship is falling apart but she hasn't taken it off your closet door. Oh, and I can't leave out your varsity jacket still on your chair. And then there's your graduation picture. When Mom sees it she practically weeps, smiles, and says how handsome you are. Hence, the Shrine of Angus."

"What can I say? I'm so deserving you must bow down upon entrance."

"Yah right."

"Hey, before I forget, how's Bryan doing?" Angus inquired about her husband adding, "When does he get back from his deployment?"

"I am so excited. I can hardly wait to see him. It's been a year. He'll be home in thirty-two days and fourteen hours, but that can always change. You sure you don't want to move back home?"

"There's no way I'm moving back home. There's no way my 6'2" frame will fit my old twin bed. Besides, we both know their one rule."

In unison they said, "If you stay at home, you have to go to church."

"And there is no way I'm doing that. I have to go. Talk to you later, sister pants."

"Errr, you know I hate that nickname."

"Bye."

Chapter 2

It took Clara almost a month before she found a rental place for Angus. Someone at church said to ask Grammie and her brother, Willard. Clara and Angus loved Grammie; cranky yet humorous, she always spoke her mind in a stern yet loving way. Grammie was the church's elderly mascot so to speak. She could be found most mornings— her afternoons were reserved for napping—at Mount Hope praying, pacing, stomping, and storming the gates of hell on behalf of each prayer request submitted every Sunday. As a faithful member of Mount Hope Church since 1950 she never missed a service unless she was ill.

Somehow, to everybody at Mount Hope, she became known as Grammie.

As children, Angus and Clara stopped by her house on the way home from school for one of her gooey oatmeal raisin cookies and to chat about the day's events and play with her cats.

"Hello, Grammie, how are you doing today?" Clara asked getting out of her car.

"Fine, sweetie," Grammie replied as she kneeled squirting weed killer on her lawn with diabolical precision. "I'm going to rid my lawn of crabgrass and sticker burrs if it's the last thing I do. Oh, these old bones, could you help me up, please?" Grammie said, struggling to her feet while rubbing her back.

"Sure, one of Mom's friends said to check with you, said you might be interested in renting the apartment above your garage?"

"Well now, these days it's hard to find good renters, besides it hasn't been cleaned in ages. Willard and I haven't gone up there in years. We nearly killed each other waiting for the house to be renovated. Our parents left us a mess. It needed new plumbing, electrical, and carpet. I've heard horror stories about renters. Do you know Mrs. White had a renter who flushed kitty litter down the toilet? Turned to cement it did."

Clara tried to wait patiently as Grammie continued on, but decided to interrupt her. "It's a reliable renter. It's Angus, he's moving back to town and needs a place."

"Oh my. What good news. Your mom must be overjoyed."

"She's pretty excited, Grammie, but also disappointed he isn't moving back in."

"Willard," Grammie hollered at her brother, who was watching from behind the screen door. "Willard you know where the apartment keys are?"

"No, old woman, I don't," he shouted.

"Hold on here, Clara. I'll go get the key. My good-for-nothing brother couldn't find a hole in the ground if he stepped in it."

Clara chuckled and walked around to the garage and appreciated Grammie's green thumb. While she waited, she admired the yellow pansies, white daisies, red hibiscus with large frail crepe paper flowers the size of saucers, and salvia planted along the sidewalk leading to the apartment.

Clara followed Grammie up the steep, weather-worn wooden steps. Grammie jiggled the key in the lock and unlocked the rusty door. The door creaked open revealing an apartment preserved in its original 1970's condition.

Clara looked about and noted the living room was huge, taking up nearly half of the second floor over the garage.

Walking around, she opened doors, and asked, "Does the furniture stay? I know Angus will like the authentic retro 1960s and 1970s look. He'll love the orange velvet supersize sofa!" Clara exclaimed. She sat on the couch causing a cloud of dust to erupt, making her sneeze. She paused and appreciated the chunky barrel leather chair and the two-foot lava lamp.

"Oh, wow, what a lamp. Does it work?"

"Did when we last lived here," Grammie said.

"And the dining room table, it's Formica and aluminum," Clara commented while writing her name in the dust. "Hey, Grammie, I think you'd better water the plant," Clara said pointing to the standing white plastic terrarium with long dead plants still in it.

"Sweetheart, Willard and I have no use for these old things, course the furniture stays."

"What do you think you'd rent it for?"

"Well, seeing as how it's Angus, I'd rent it for $700 a month, and that includes water and trash. He'd have to pay for his own electric."

"It's a deal. Looks like you have a renter. I will come by this weekend to get the key and clean it up."

***

Angus pulled into the driveway in front of his new apartment and parked beneath a tattered basketball hoop.

Grammie waited at the bottom of the steps. She greeted him with a huge hug and said, "Angus, so glad to have you back. You holler if you need anything. I made you a nice dinner plate, warm chicken casserole, and biscuits. It's in the microwave. I'll come by tomorrow, and we can settle up then."

"Thanks, Grammie," he said, returning the hug. "See you tomorrow."

Angus lifted a cardboard box of dilapidated and worn unmatched kitchen utensils and other items from his car and lugged it up the steps. He opened the door surveying the place. "Not too bad, Clara. It's kinda cool," he mused aloud.

"The place certainly is musty. Love the old wood flooring and wow what a huge living room. The picture window is as wide as the worn sofa." He ran his hands over the stained couch. "Yikes, gotta get it cleaned."

He walked over to the kitchen where an enormous dusty wooden fork and spoon hung on vintage green and gold stock pot and fruited wallpaper. *Never liked those things, kinda creepy.* As a boy he expected a giant to be lurking around waiting to use the fork and spoon, served up with a sound heaping of unruly kid! He shuddered and caught sight of the metal sunburst golden clock covered in cobwebs tucked in the corner near the stove. *Clara, looks like you forgot to clean the clock.*

He opened the mushroom canister set on the counter and saw Grammie had filled each with flour, sugar, tea, and ground coffee.

"Grammie, you're too good," Angus said taking a whiff of the coffee. He spotted the TV, radio, and record player console combo. "Awesome." Lifting the doily, he opened it and saw an old Simon and Garfunkel album and a Charley Pride 8-track. "Hmm, guess I'll have to give these to Grammie, certainly not my taste."

A large avocado green sink and shower filled the tiny bathroom. He took a few steps and turned to see an empty bedroom. *Guess I gotta buy me a bed and dresser. I think I can find those at the secondhand store and pick up a new mattress. Easy peasy.*

Angus glanced out the large living room window. *Glad I can park the Bronco in the garage.* He smiled when he remembered how Grammie forced Willard to relinquish his driver's license after he confused the brake pedal with the gas pedal and ran their old green Buick into the side of the church when he was supposed to be picking up Grammie after service.

I'd better thank Clara big time for this. He continued unpacking the box. And cleaned for the remainder of the day.

Chapter 3

Let beer be for those who are perishing,
wine for those who are in anguish!
Let them drink and forget their poverty
and remember their misery no more. Proverbs 31:6-7 (NIV)

Angus enjoyed the drive through town on his way to work. A cool crisp autumn morning greeted him when he stepped outside. The air smelled clean and slapped his face when he stepped outside in the sun.

He reached the town square and saw few changes. The old Ritz theater marquee advertised the latest hit movie. Crepe myrtle trees dropped their blooms of pink and white blossoms, some floating through the air like tiny bits of cotton candy. Park benches intermittently spotted the grass, providing rest for those in need.

The stately brick and mortar seven-story courthouse—designated a historic landmark a few years back—dominated the center of the town. It reminded him of a Norman Rockwell painting. Angus knew beneath the paint there was a darker side to small-town life: people in pain, biting gossips, lowlife wife beaters, jockeying of and manipulation of small-town politics, and petty larceny. Judging by the graffiti on the side of the bank, gangs and drugs were digging their claws into Riverside.

He drove slowly around the square through the second stoplight, and two blocks later pulled into the old library, now the police station and jail. Funny how the smell of old books still lingered in the air causing Angus to stifle a sneeze when he opened the door. He took the wooden steps two at a time, landing loudly with a thump and reached the top. He hurried across the squeaky bare wood floor and opened the door to the main office area then walked over and knocked on Sheriff Rex's door.

"Enter," Sheriff Rex bellowed.

"Hello, Rex," Angus said and shook his hand, thinking about how Rex wore his badge with authority and compassion. He knew Rex well enough from the stories his dad told about him. Built like Hoss from the old Bonanza TV series, Rex could be congenial, but if you lied to him, he would be as unforgiving as yoga pants on a sumo wrestler.

"Thanks for the job. It sure is great to be back home and—"

"Hold that thought, Angus." Rex stood and interrupted him, motioning for Angus to follow him. They walked out to the main common area lined with desks.

"I want to introduce you to the team. These here are the three jail cells, we book 'em and put 'em here, and if needed send the worst offenders over to the county seat if the charges are serious." He turned and adjusted his heavy service belt. "Usually, it's full on holidays with those who drank too much and come summertime we get the occasional teen shoplifting. Nothing too serious. Your desk is here right next to the window."

Angus looked down at the ancient wooden desk and could've sworn he saw old Mrs. Wallace sitting there studying the Dewey Decimal catalog cards. He smiled but was pulled from his thoughts.

Rex motioned with his head and a short, stocky man with a muscular frame stood to greet Angus.

"This is Mark Foreman. He's new to the force, fresh outta the academy," Rex said.

The two shook hands. Angus noted he was powerfully built—a solid wall of muscle stood before him. It was plain Mark went to the gym a lot.

"And this here is Shirley Striker, but we all call her Sher or Sherman, just like the tank. She's been here as long as you've been gone, six years, is that right, Sherman?"

"Yeah," she answered and walked over and shook Angus' hand firmly.

He sized her up, noticing her figure was more angular than curvy, not his type. Looking at her he knew the moniker of a Sherman tank fit her well. Before him stood a woman, who could roll over and crush any criminal. *She's gotta be the biggest, strongest woman I've ever seen. She'd make a great pro wrestler.* I'd better step up my workouts. Sherman's dull brown hair contrasted with her piercing blue eyes. Eyes the color of an angry ocean, eyes that taunted and said "pick a fight, any fight, and I will kick your ass."

Rex pointed to the desk near the door and said, "Over there is Jean. If you need the scoop about anyone in town, she's your go-to, and yes, she is as cranky as she looks."

"Thanks. I think," Jean said. She stood, smiled and reached across the desk to shake hands with Angus. Brushing back her unruly gray hair she said, "If I am cranky it comes from dealing with you yokels here." She gave Rex a sneer and stuck the latest call info in his hand and squeezed into her chair. She gave a short grunt and turned back to her National Enquire magazine.

Rex looked at the note she handed him and said, "Oh damn, it's Macey, again. How is it this time of year always creeps up on us? Same thing every July and September."

Angus scratched his head. *Macey? Nah, it can't be. I haven't seen her since we split up.*

"Sherman, you and Angus can handle this one. It'll be good to get him acquainted with the town jumper."

"Okay, but do you mind if I drive, Sher? Can I call you Sher or do like Sherman better?"

"Sher is fine. I don't care, you can drive," she said and handed him the squad car keys.

"Where to?"

"The Rivanna River Bridge off 64. Do you know where it is?"

"Sure do."

On the drive over, Sherman filled Angus in on Macey and how every year on July 10 and September 19 she gets three sheets to the wind drunk and attempts suicide. Attempts because the bridge isn't far above the water, but with the recent rains the undertow in certain places could drag a person under.

"Hey, what's Macey's last name?"

"Wilson."

"I was afraid it was her. She was my high school sweetheart. We go way back. I've known her since grade school. And I think I know exactly why she picked todays date."

She tilted her head to one side and asked, "Really? Why?"

"Never mind, I'll tell you later," Angus rolled the car to a slow stop next to Macey's old and dented brown two-door pickup. The copper rust covered the truck, making it hard to tell where the rust began and the brown paint ended.

"Okay, since you know her, I'll let you take the lead on this one."

He and Sherman got out of the squad car and cautiously walked to the solitary figure on the old trestle bridge. Traffic stopped in both directions.

Macey turned to Angus as he walked towards her. Slurring her words, she staggered and said, "Angish, ish that you?"

"Hey, Macey, what's going on? What are you doing out here?"

"Oh, Angish, you came back! A little late don't ya think? Clara said you'd be here. I even did my makeup jush for you. Like it?" she said hiccupping.

Her appearance startled him, and he took a step back before saying, "Uh, yah, Macey, you look outstanding," when in reality except for her high cheekbones and black hair Angus hardly recognized her.

She looked like a demented peacock with blue, green, and gold eye shadow smeared across her eyes.

Rivers of black mascara and eyelash globs stuck to her face like little, fuzzy caterpillars. She looked quite a sight standing there, her petite frame swallowed up in her PJ's.

He stepped closer. "Macey, come away from the edge."

"Why? You don't care," she whined.

"Of course I do." Trying to distract her he asked, "Whatcha got in your hand?"

"It's my Jose Cuervo Margarita Tequila mixt." She giggled. "Jose hesh a mine friend. Want some?" She staggered toward him holding the bottle high in the air.

He inched closer to her. "Nah, sorry, I am on the job."

Sherman came up behind Angus and whispered, "Geez, Angus, what'd you do to her?"

Macey tried to take a long swig but missed her mouth, causing the drink to run down her neck onto her hot pink camo PJ top.

Angus stepped nearer. *I can't believe what I'm seeing.* He raised his shades up and down a few times. *Is that peanut butter and fruit loops in her messy hair?* He moved in closer. *Lordy, she smells like puke and alcohol. Definitely, not peanut butter in the hair.*

She took another long sloshy swig, again getting the drink on her neck, top, and chest.

"Oops, guesh I'd better take this old thing off." She dropped her head and with great concentration she ever so slowly unbuttoned her top, revealing the sports bra underneath. Then she waved the shirt in the air and dropped it into the swift-running muddy water below. She leaned over the bridge railing, giggled and said, "Bye, bye pinky, winky shirpty, I meant shirty!"

Angus stared at her chest as a group of teens behind him whistled from their dented and variously colored rusted out Franken truck. Knife marks, little rail road-type crisscross carvings, covered her chest and abdomen.

"Hey Sher, get a blanket please."

"Sure thing, there should be one in the trunk. I'm on it." She turned and ran to the cruiser.

"I hate these things, they're so itchy," he said and took the blanket.

"You like my belly, Angush?" Macey asked as she traced the outline of the cuts with her free hand. "Ain't my drawings purty? My share-a-pist, I mean therapisht says I'm a cutter."

She stared long and hard at Angus, turning her head side to side. She burped, stumbled and lurched, then bowing deeply, lost her balance and passed out on the concrete. The bottle splintering into glass shards beside her.

Angus put the blanket over her. He picked her up being careful to not reinjure his back and carried her to the squad car.

Walking to the car, he heard retching, and before he laid her down, she puked all over his brand new, first-day on the job crisply ironed uniform.

Sherman quickly opened door, and Angus placed Macey in the backseat, then got behind the wheel. Not wanting to get puke everywhere, he asked Sherman, "After you call the station, can you call my sister, Clara? My phone is on the dash."

While driving, he explained that Clara and Macey had been best friends forever and that Macey owns and

operates the pet grooming place behind his sister's veter-
inarian clinic. He added, "Man, she reeks. Let's get her to
Clara. I really don't want to smell her at the station. She
can take care of her." Thinking he'd never been able to do
that back in Chicago. Realizing small-town stations had
more liberty as long as you didn't do anything drastic.

"Hello?"

"Hello, is this Clara?"

"Yes."

"This is Sherman with Riverside PD. I have you on
the speakerphone. Your brother has Macey passed out in
the back of the squad car."

"Oh no! Is today the nineteenth?"

"Yup."

"I completely forgot. Tell Angus I will meet you
both at the back door."

"Okay, be there in a few." Sherman ended the call
and said, "Now, please tell me what this is all about.
She's been doing this since I've been here, and that's
been years."

"I'll fill you in on the way to Clara's."

Chapter 4

There is a way that appears to be right,
but in the end, it leads to death.
Proverbs 14:12 (NIRV)

"Okay, the July jumping thing is the month we split up. We were seniors in high school, and she told me she was pregnant. We were going to get married, but I got an anonymous note saying she wasn't pregnant. I showed the note to my buddies and my football coach, and they said she's playing me and she probably isn't pregnant. So, I broke it off and didn't talk to her again until now. The September 19 date, today, is the day I left for the academy. It must have affected her a lot more than I ever thought possible."

Clara's house was a few miles away, and the rest of the short ride was quiet except for the occasional groans emanating from Macey.

Angus pulled the squad car around back into their grandparent's old house. Clara got the small cottage bungalow for a steal when they passed away. White shiplap siding and black shutter trim complimented the decorative picket fence out front. The open front porch led to an old wood door adorned with a fan stained glass window and glass doorknob. Several mature maple trees graced the chain link fenced yard keeping her two behemoth dogs contained.

Angus parked the cruiser in the driveway. He leaned in and lifted Macey out of the back seat. His back spasmed. He'd pay for this later.

The carpet of yellow and orange maple leaves crackled like flames as Angus and Sherman held Macey and walked across the deck and into Clara's house.

"Geez, Macey's a heavy little thing, for all her dead weight," Sherman said as Macey's legs buckled.

Angus banged on the door.

"All right, I can hear you. I'm right here," Clara hollered as she rushed to open the back door. She dressed quickly, pulled her hair back into a tight ponytail. Bangs graced her face, and a stubborn cowlick poked through creating a bump. She wore her husband's old green work shirt. It complimented her long mahogany colored hair and dark brown eyes. "Take her to the bathroom and lay her in the tub."

Angus scooped Macey up and hopscotched across the wooden floor, stepping around the cowhide rug, dog bones, and past the leather sofa. He glanced at himself in the bathroom mirror, and noted he needed to get his disobedient brown hair cut. He maneuvered Macey around the shower doors and softly laid her in the tub and turned on the warm water.

"Man, sis, I had no idea she was that torn up about the breakup and me going to the academy."

Clara raised her eyebrows took a deep breath and looked at her puked-on brother and said, "Uh, what? You think she gets drunk and cuts herself because of *you*? Hate to burst your prideful bubble, but you sure ain't all that. You certainly esteem yourself higher than you should. Geez, Angus, she drinks and cuts herself because it's the anniversary of her abortion, you idiot. When she had the abortion, she quit going to church and hasn't been in years even though I keep asking her to go. And to top it off, she dates jerks because she's convinced it's what she deserves."

He stiffened, blinked and shook his head. "Her what? She wasn't pregnant."

"Oh yes she was. She kept hoping you wouldn't leave, but you did. Mom and Dad were so disappointed you left her. They begged her not to do it, showed her what the 'procedure' was, and told her she could stay with them. Macey wouldn't have it. She didn't want to be another poor Native American destitute teen mom. So, she had the abortion the day you left town."

Shocked, Angus hung his head. "I didn't know, sis. I didn't know."

"Well, I tried to tell you, several times, you'd only tell me to shut up, yelling she's a liar, you didn't want to talk about her. I left a note on your pillow, and you wadded it up tossed it in the trash without reading it."

Bracing himself against the bathroom counter, Angus let the news sink in. He slowly opened the bathroom door and headed back to the squad car where Sherman sat listening to the radio traffic.

On the way out he doubled over and stared in disgust as Brutus and Bullet, Clara's two mastiff mixed-breed mutts, licked up the vomit from the blanket. He wondered why Clara and his mom gave their dogs the same names. When a dog died, the new one got the same name, it was so confusing. He gripped a chair and gagged, wondering if the sight of the dogs eating the puke made him nauseous or if what he learned made him sick.

He slid in behind the steering wheel, shut the door quietly, pushed against the headrest, and groaned.

"Well? What happened? What's going on?" Sherman asked as she twisted around to see Angus. He retold everything to her and when he finished, she sucked in a breath. "Wow, what a shocker. You had no idea?"

"No, I had no idea, and I don't want to talk about it," he snapped, thinking he would have a long talk with his parents on his first day off.

Chapter 5

*Those who think they know something do not
yet know as they ought to know.
I Corinthians 8:2 (NIV)*

Angus lay in his bed awake all night, twisting, tossing and untucking the blankets, rehearsing the taxing conversation he was going to have with his folks.

He thought about how he hated talking with them, how every conversation revolved around God.

"Mom, how are things going?"

"Great, we're blessed."

"Mom, Dad, I need some advice."

"Well, you know, son, trust in the Lord with all your heart, and he will direct your path."

"On and on they'd drone about God." He grumbled in the dark bedroom. "They didn't get it. I don't want anything to do with a deity that allowed Mr. Jones, the church deacon, to molest my best friend Kolby. No sir, not gonna worship a god that let Uncle Robert, the head usher, leave his wife and kids for the church secretary. Nope, not a god I want any part of."

He fumed and fussed with his pillow punching it, recalling how tongues wagged, once the high and mighty Mrs. Grobbels spread the word about his uncle. She caused quite a stir in the congregation and in the community. The stench of his uncle's sin lingered over each member of his family like a trash truck. The noxious smell of it clung to them, and seeped into the fabric of their everyday lives. He knew these two incidents obliterated his faith, it caused anger, weeds of bitterness, and unforgiveness to grow and overtake the garden of life God planted in him long ago.

How can my folks continue to attend that rinky-dink backward Mount Hope Church?

Angus rolled over, and his mind returned to Macey and the abortion; furious with his parents and angry with himself at the same time. He glared at the alarm clock and made a mental list of questions to ask them. *When were you going to tell me? Were you afraid of the scandal? Did you even encourage her to adopt out my child, your grandchild?*

Agitated he stared at the alarm clock—it showed 4 a.m. The alarm went off at 6:30 a.m. with a loud ear-punishing bell. Angus slammed the clock down with such force he dented the decorative metal top of the nightstand.

He showered, slapping himself awake as the hot water washed over him. To save time, he brushed his teeth while showering. Looking around he got the cleanest dirty towel he could find on the floor, regretting his decision to wad them up and pack them dirty. He wiped off and dressed quickly, then splashed on cologne to combat the towel's mildew odor. He wanted to talk with his folks before they started their Bible time; the less he heard about God the better.

Angus tried to contain himself and not speed on his way to his parents' place. On the way, he remembered the happy times in his childhood, in the one hundred-plus-year-old house a few homes down from his sister's place. He remembered the times he and his dad refinished the floors, and worked on the 1971 two-door Chevy Nova—his first car. For a moment he smiled and thought of times spent talking of school, football, and girls. His mind drifted to Macey and the abortion, which caused him to scowl and his thoughts to turn dark.

Maples, oaks, and pines lined his parents' street. Picket fences and little dogs looking out living room windows lined the avenue.

Their house had a detached slanting roof garage used for garden tools and lawn supplies. The riding lawn mower gave it a motor oil and gasoline smell. A dusty grill leaned against the wall near a torn bag of crumbling charcoal.

He pulled into the drive and shook his head to clear his thoughts. Then got out of his beat-up blue and white Bronco and shut the door with malice.

The garage door was half open. He peeked in to see tools lying on the wooden work bench next to small piles of sawdust. *Dad never puts away the tools.* His mom's ginormous collection of Christmas lawn ornaments, baby Jesus, stars, and halo-less angels all competed for storage space with Santa and Rudolf.

Angus took a deep breath; when he exhaled, the crisp autumn air caused his breath to rise like smoke from an angry dragon's mouth. He retucked his shirt into his pants and stomped across the deck preparing for a tense and touchy conversation.

***

Anne stood by the kitchen window. She closed her eyes, remembering as she admired the magnolia tree the kids had planted near the kitchen for Mother's Day years ago.

"You remember how we took the kids camping way back when?"

Will folded the morning paper. "Sure do. Remember the time Angus told us about his teacher?"

"How could I forget? I sometimes wonder if what happened then is the cause of his false bravado." She wiped her hands on the towel, paused and thought back, lost in time gazing out the window.

Anne smiled and said, "Boys, girls, get in the car. It's time to go."

Clara and her two friends, Macey and Belissa, along with Angus and his friend, Kolby, said in unison, "Yes, ma'am," as they piled into the minivan.

"Brutus, hop in the back with Angus and Kolby," Will said.

Brutus obeyed and leapt into the back.

"Gee, Dad, does the dog have to ride with us?" Angus protested.

"For someone going camping, you sure are doing a lot of complaining," Will said as Anne nodded in agreement.

"He's been mean to me all day," Clara declared from the middle seat.

"Have not."

"Have too."

"Have not."

"Have too."

"All right, stop it. Let's get going," Will said in exasperation, shutting the van hatchback door. "Okay, girls, lift your feet. I need to find a spot for the groceries."

The girls complied and automatically lifted their feet as they continued posing their Barbie dolls lost in play.

Sliding in behind the steering wheel, he said, "And we're off. It's going to be a great getaway weekend," as he looked in the rearview mirror.

Each of the girls played with their dolls as a curious Anne listened from the front seat.

"I'm going to marry Angus," Belissa said. "He's so cute."

"*Ewww*! He is not! He's gross," Clara shouted. "He picks his nose, *and* he eats his boogers!"

"Do not!" Angus protested.

"Do too." Clara hollered.

"Do not!"

"Do too!"

"Mom, make her stop, I'd never marry you, Belissa Baker. You're ugly!"

"Angus Allen Connors, you apologize right this instant. What a horrible thing to say," Anne said.

"Oh, all right. Sorry, Belissa, but all girls are ugly!"

"It's okay, it's true," Belissa said as she wiped away a tear.

"No, it isn't," Anne said trying to console her as she patted Belissa's knee.

"Geez, what's gotten into him?" Will asked. "He's been in such a rotten mood these past few days. I hoped a trip to the cabin would get him out of his funk."

"Mom, Brutus keeps farting!" Angus hollered.

"Good boy, Brutus," Will said laughing, "Now you truly have something to complain about."

"Hey, Angus, stop hitting me," Kolby exclaimed, "Mrs. Connors, can I go home? He's being mean."

"Sorry, honey, but we're a few minutes from the cabin."

"Hey give me my book. Angus stop it, it's mine!" Kolby screamed as Angus wrestled the book from him and threw it across the back of the van.

"Stupid reading, it's all you ever do!"

"It's not stupid."

"Yes, it is!" Angus folded his arms across his chest.

"Angus Allen Connors, I am going to pull over now, and we can go switch hunting! You apologize this instant!" Will said watching from the rearview mirror.

"Yes, sir," Angus crossed his arms, huffed and without looking Kolby in the face said, "Sorry, Kolby. What ya reading about anyway?"

"Planets."

"Planets? That's boring."

"No, it's not. Did you know there is a butt planet?"

Angus' eyes widened in wonder. "Really?"

"Yah, it's called Uranus. Get it? Your anus!"

Both boys laughed uproariously as Will chuckled and said to Anne, "I guess all little boys giggle when they hear that." He pulled the car into the gravel driveway.

"We're here!" Clara shouted.

Instantly the kids piled out of the van like clowns in a stuffed mini circus car.

"Hey, each of you, grab something." Will ordered.

Once inside Anne announced, "Okay, everyone, let's go for a swim!"

"Yippee!"

Each ran to their respective shared bedrooms and quickly changed into their bathing suits.

Will grabbed Angus. "Not so fast, young man. Let's go for a walk first."

"Do I have to, Dad?"

"Yes, son you do."

"Yes, sir," Angus answered and hung his head.

They walked down the thick tree-lined dirt road, Angus kicking at rocks with his toes and occasionally stooping to pick one up and toss into the bushes.

"Angus, let's take a seat over there on the log. See it next to the dock?"

Will strode over as Angus ambled behind him.

Angus stood at the shoreline skipping stones across the pond, looking sad and despondent.

Will sat and prayed silently, asking God for guidance. He knew something was bothering Angus, he didn't know what.

"Dad?"

"Yes, son?"

"Am I stupid?"

"Are you stupid? That's an odd question. You're *not* stupid. Why would you say that?"

"I hate school, Dad. Every day teacher makes me read in front of the class for 'practice.' When I can't say the words, she thumps her finger on my head and says over and over, 'Think, Angus, think.' Then everyone laughs. I am really trying, but it's so hard. I heard her tell Mrs. Johnston across the hall I had something wrong with me, and I'm stupid."

"Son, come here, sit down." He patted the log and gave him a big hug. "You're the smartest kid I know. Who else can keep up with Kolby? I watched you show him how to take a bike apart and put it back together. God loves you. You're fearfully and wonderfully made. Hey, I have an idea. How about you and I sneak into town and get a banana split?"

"Can we?" Angus squealed and jumped.

"Sure, race you to the road! Last one there sleeps with Brutus!"

After a dinner of roasted hot dogs, chips and s'mores, the kids ran through the front yard chasing each other and the evasive fireflies darting across the cool evening sky while Will and Anne watched from the porch swing.

"I love the peace up here," Anne said. "You should've heard the conversation Macey and I had today. She says and does the craziest and sweetest things."

"Okay, tell me."

"She came over and tugged my arm while the others were swimming and said, 'Mrs. Connors, can Angus have two wives?' Then she showed me her Skipper doll. Remember the one the boys tried to burn the hair off of?"

"Yah, I remember, what a day. I'll never forget Angus and Kolby roasting the doll on the BBQ before dinner. Geez, those two."

"Anyway, she drew a big heart on the Ken doll's head and called him Angus, and she scribbled Angus + Macey on his leg. On her Skipper doll she drew another heart on the cheek. She said she'd marry Angus when she's older, like ten. Anyway, did you find out what's bothering Angus?"

"Yup, and it's not good."

"Oh really?"

As Will recounted what Angus told him, Anne grew mad, her righteous indignation boiled over, erupting into a verbal tirade as she fumed.

Standing, she placed her hands on her hips. "She said what? Why the snotty little uppity fresh out of college twerp. What does she know?" She marched into the house and pulled the suitcase from under the bed and began packing their things.

"We're leaving, now, right now, so I can call the principal and that horrid teacher. How dare she! Angus is *the* sweetest. He begged me to buy her Valentines chocolates. He's always respectful to her. I tell you what, I'll give her a piece of my mind. I'll smack her into next week. Saying my son is stupid." She shoved clothing into the tattered suitcase. "Telling him to think! Why I'll make her *think* twice about humiliating my son. Kids," she screamed as she dragged the old leather suitcase down the hall and to the car, "Kids we're leaving now!" She jerked the car door open, "Get in the car."

"Honey, quiet down," Will hurried to keep pace with her, trying unsuccessfully to remove the suitcase from her firm white knuckled grip.

"Why are we leaving, Dad? We just got here."

"We not leaving, son. Now go back and play."

"Simmer down, Anne. This can wait until Monday," Will said taking the suitcase from her. "Wait till Monday. It'll give you time to calm down and for us to pray. Let's try to find something Angus likes and he's good at to instill confidence in him."

"Oh, all right, I suppose you're right. But we will still have a come to Jesus meeting when I get back."

"I know Anne, I know."

"He mentioned something the other day about Pee Wee football. You think he'd be good at sports?" Anne asked.

"Don't see why not. He's huge for his age, taller and bigger than the other boys in his class."

Anne was jarred from reminiscing as Angus pulled in the driveway.

She sighed and said, "I wonder what ever happened to the polite, sweet, humble little boy of mine?"

"Over confidence in his intellect and abilities, that's what happened," Will replied.

Angus hollered and blew in the back door. "Mom, Dad, where are you? We need to talk." He walked through the kitchen past Brutus number six. *What is it with his mom and sister loving big slobbery dogs?*

For the first time, he visited his parents' house early in the morning before their Bible study.

"We're in here son," his mom said.

She gave him a hug, smiled, and asked, "Can I get you some eggs and turkey bacon?"

His dad interrupted his thoughts, "You do *not* want to eat the turkey bacon, son. It's like painted meat, and the Paleo gluten-free bread tastes like flavored sand. Geez, I hate it when your mom puts me on another diet."

"Sit down, son. At least let me get you some coffee."

"No thanks, Mom."

"Don't bother," his dad said. "It's decaf, another new healthy diet idea."

"I don't want coffee, and I don't want to sit. We need to talk," Angus said tersely.

Will and Anne exchanged looks and Angus sensed they thought this was going to be another of his outbursts blaming them for something. But that wasn't going to happen, not this time. He'd grown since he left Riverside. They seemed to be holding their breath. His mom caressed the cross necklace probably praying for wisdom. He didn't care, it was a bunch of baloney to him.

"Listen, I'm just going to rip the bandage off. When'd you find out Macey was pregnant and got an abortion? How come you didn't tell me?"

"Well, son," his dad replied, running his hands through his short gray hair, "if you remember, you weren't the easiest person to get along with then. You kept running from God, always gone when we left for work, and you came home very late every night. We tried. Anytime we were able to talk with you, it turned into a screaming match and ended with you calling us 'sheeple' saying we're like sheep being led to a slaughter following anyone with a Bib—"

Angus interrupted his dad before he could get all preachy. "Didn't you try to stop her and offer more help?"

His dad pushed his plate of food away from the table and stood.

"You're getting way out of line here."

His mom took Angus' hand. "Honey, sit down and let us explain."

"No!" Angus pounded his fist on the table. "Tell me now. I need to know."

"Well," his dad said. "It was your senior year, and you lived, ate and breathed football and partying. You weren't here much, and anytime we tried to talk with you about Macey, you exploded and said you wanted nothing more to do with her. You called her nasty names I can't even repeat. It broke our hearts to know you thought that of her."

"I'm sure those same words ran through your and Mom's minds. Don't deny it."

"I am going to deny it. We loved Macey and still do."

Angus gripped the table, and wondered aloud, "How could she do such a thing to our baby?"

"We tried to talk her out of the abortion. We even opened our house to her, but she was determined she wasn't going to raise another child on the reservation, especially not living in poverty with her alcoholic grandfather in a rundown trailer with no electric or heat. Do you really think we wanted her to abort our *grandchild*? Do you truly believe as Christians we'd turn her out? Is that what you think of us and God?"

"Don't bring God into this." Angus tightened his jaw, and spoke through clenched teeth. "Geez, can't we have at least one conversation without bringing God into it? Can we for once not get churchy?"

"Well, yes, we can, but you can't get more churchy than a life and death situation, and I *am* going to bring God into this conversation."

Angus paused. He knew his dad was right, but he wasn't going to admit it.

"Son," his mom said tenderly as she touched his arm, "please stop running from God."

Angus jerked his arm away. The hurt cut deep, and he struggled to hold back tears of regret.

"Hate to tell you this, Dad, Mom, but I'm on a sabbatical from God." Angus picked up his keys, stomping as he left the house, slamming the door behind him.

His dad sighed and said, "Anne, the brilliance of his stupidity is only outshined by his capacity for arrogance. Lord, please continue to work on him."

Chapter 6

*For if you forgive other people when
they sin against you, your heavenly
Father will also forgive you.
But if you do not forgive others their sins,
your Father will not forgive your sins.
Matthew 6:14–15 (NIV)*

Angus needed a long slow drive to digest the conversation at his folks' house. Deciding to take advantage of the warm weather, and figuring a lengthy walk would help him clear his head, he pulled up at the Rivanna Hiking Trail.

Moms with baby strollers, kids on tricycles, and the occasional elderly couple holding hands passed by. He wondered how people survive marriage and stay together for the long haul. Though he tried, Angus couldn't keep a relationship beyond six months. If it happened to last through the fall, he broke it off so he didn't have to buy a piece of jewelry, giving the wrong impression.

With his head down he strode, determination in his steps and was roused from his thoughts when he spotted a pretty, petite woman walking by. Turning, he smiled when he saw Belissa, Macey's and Clara's childhood friend.

Batting her eyelashes, she said in sugary, southern drawl, "Angus, honey, is that you? Whatever are you doing back in town? You're as handsome and fit as ever."

"Hey, Belissa how are you?" he said, trying hard to not stare at her sleeve tattoos. Except for the black goats with red eyes, upside-down crosses, and pentagram tattoos on her right arm, he thought she looked great. She hadn't changed much; the tats were a new addition to her china doll complexion that complimented her almost blue-black hair and green eyes.

They continued to exchange the usual pleasantries, inquiring about each other's parents and jobs.

"Hey, you want to see a movie Friday? I'll pick you up at six, and we can grab a quick bite and head over to the theater after we eat."

"Why, Angus, I'd love to." She walked her fingers up his arm, and smiled coyly. "I truly want to stay and chat, but I have to finish my jog. Gotta keep my figure, you know. I live above Joey's BBQ. It's also where I work," she added, then blew him a kiss and jogged off.

Angus grinned and admired the view as she jogged away. "It's hotter than Hades out here." He wiped the sweat from his brow and got in the car. *Too hot to walk that's for sure. I need some groceries may as well stop by the store.* He pulled in and thought he saw Kolby coming out of the Piggly Wiggly. *Yup, it's him, I'd know his long stride and red hair anywhere.*

Angus parked, got out and placed his foot on the bumper of the Bronco. "Well, if it ain't the block of cheese."

"Man, please stop calling me that name. How many times do I have to tell you it's Colby with a 'K'? You idiot cow." Kolby said walking up to Angus.

"Um, that's a bull, as in you mess with the bull you get the horns."

"You have to stop saying that. It's so old-farty."

"Whatever, dude," Angus replied. He pulled out some gum and said, "Hey, block o' cheese, gotta minute?"

"Yah, sure, I have about fifteen minutes until Tonya finishes her manicure. I'm picking up a few things for her family cookout later on. They want to have one more get together before it turns too cold."

"Okay. I'll be quick. I was wondering how you and your parents moved on after what happened to you when we were kids? You know, get over it?"

"What made you think of that? I try to forget about it. It's not something I will ever completely get over, but I have moved on. Jones is in jail, miserable, and I have forgiven him."

Angus cocked his head, blinking rapidly. "What? Forgiven him?"

"Yah, it took a while, and after years of rebelling, you know how I was. You were my partner in crime, ditching school, smoking pot with me, stealing sodas from the 7-11, making fun of the Barker twins for saving themselves for marriage. Man, we were merciless. Funny, now I'm a Christian." He paused and scanned the parking lot for signs of Tonya.

"Anyway, you were always smarter and never got caught. You stayed home and skipped breaking into the school with me and trashing Principal Watson's office with toilet paper, string confetti, and stinky fish spray. That was the last straw seeing as how I was just suspended for setting off smoke bombs in the bathrooms and pulling the fire alarms. Of course, I got caught."

"Yah, I remember, you're lucky you didn't go to juvie."

"Well, it woke me up."

Incredulous, Angus crossed his arms. "Didn't you want revenge?"

"Sure, I did. Did I ever tell you what happened when Sheriff Rex brought Mr. Jones in after he found the pictures on his computer and arrested him?"

"No, you didn't tell me."

"It's not something I should talk about, and you'll know why when I finish. You have to promise to never tell *anyone* what I am going to say. Okay?"

"Of course, fire away, bud."

"I have to tell you Sheriff Rex was all over Mr. Jones. He deduced he was lying when he interrogated him. Man, he caught the scent of Mr. Jones' lies and tracked down the truth like a bloodhound. I was sitting at Deputy Dawg Daniels' desk. Remember how his face sagged and his jowls made him look like a bloodhound? Anyway, he was a nice man, truly compassionate. He died last year."

"I didn't know that."

"Okay, I'd better hurry. So, I'm at his desk when Sheriff Rex brought Mr. Jones in, tosses him in the cell, and slammed the cell door shut so hard the station door glass rattled. Then he calmly and methodically went to each window and pulled the shades down, and he turns the radio on super loud, some stupid boy band song was playing. He tosses a twenty at Jean and told her to take a long lunch. He goes down the hall and opens the door and get this your mom, my mom and Grammie came walking in. My dad must have been working, he wasn't with them. Right away, Deputy Dawg turned and tried to steer my eyes away by showing me a *Car and Driver* magazine on his desk.

"With great deliberation and calm the sheriff took Mr. Jones from the cell and put him in the smelly storage closet in the old library. Remember the one we used to sneak in to view the girly magazines the janitor stashed there?"

"Yeah, what happened?" Angus snapped his fingers impatiently.

"I'm getting to it. Well, then the sheriff takes the three ladies to the closet, shuts the door, and walks over to the radio and turns it up even louder, so loud the windows shook and I put my hands over my ears.

"Once the song finished, he strolls over to the closet, escorts them out, and thanked them for their help! He grabs a moaning, barely walking hunched over Mr. Jones. I swear there wasn't a place on his face that wasn't bloody. He held his stomach. My mom smiles, looks at me, and says 'Momma's got a dark side,' and kicks him in the gonads! That's when Jones passed out on the floor. Then Sheriff Rex and deputy Dawg dragged him to the squad car and took him to the hospital. I heard they told the nursing staff he fell going down the stairs. Back then no one talked about police brutality. I guess Mr. Jones figured he deserved what he got. I only saw Mr. Jones one more time, at his sentencing. Turns out he had done this before so the judge gave him twenty-five years. I'd say they got their pound of flesh and then some. I have never been more proud of my mom.

"Once I realized getting into trouble was getting me nowhere, I changed. I considered how Pastor Tuttle said vengeance is mine and we need to forgive, because God forgave us. It wasn't easy and it took some time, but I forgave Mr. Jones. I had to. Jesus forgave my sins so I had to forgive him. It was hard to do, but I did it. And when I am feeling especially charitable, I pray for his salvation."

Shocked, Angus said, "You what?"

"Yah, I do. Hey, here comes Tonya. I have to go."

"How you ever got her is beyond me." Angus slapped Kolby's back.

"It's my boyish charm and dancing skills." Kolby said with a sheepish grin.

"Thanks, you have given me something to think about." He'd rather think about what happened to Kolby and not think about Macey and rationalize his girl after girl, string of relationships lifestyle while trying to convince himself he was happy.

"Hi, Angus, can't talk," Tonya said. "We have to go, or we will be seriously late for our cookout. Come by sometime for dinner. Glad you're back. I know Kolby is happy too."

***

Tonya gave Kolby a quick kiss and opened the car door for her.

"What were you two discussing?" she asked.

"What happened when I was a kid."

"Oh, that. Why?"

"I guess Angus is struggling with forgiveness. He's a mess and doesn't even know it."

She scooted closer. "Hmm, enough about him. Did you buy the food for the cookout?"

"It's in the cooler. I hate these cookouts. I detest being the only white guy there. Your uncle Steve always makes rude remarks. It's uncomfortable to say the least." He started the car and drove away.

She raised her eyebrows. "Really? I have to endure your cousins and sisters talking about how white their legs are, how they wish they could tan and not burn, how they wish they had curly hair, then they look at me like they're going to get sympathy. And if that's not enough, I have to listen to Blake Shelton playing in the background! Ugh!"

Kolby chuckled. "Well we are in the South, and country music reigns supreme. As soon as we get to your folks' place, your ex Kelvin—who names their kid Kelvin anyways? What's up with that?—he will play the Electric Slide and tell me and you to get up and dance so he can watch you. He thinks I don't see him leering. You could have married him, the assistant mayor, and you chose me, a geeky, white, middle school science teacher." He leaned into her and asked, "Why *did* you marry me?"

"Well you asked first and you ain't ghetto."

"Well, neither is Kelvin."

"Uh, yes, he is. You don't know him well enough. Remember, man looks at the outward appearance, but God looks on the heart," Tonya said.

He pulled into her folks' driveway. "You sure it wasn't my hot dancing skills?" Kolby said wiggling lewdly and reached over to unbuckle his seatbelt.

"Kolby, stop it. Here comes Grammie. She will lay hands on you and *then* smack you in Jesus' name if she sees you doing that."

"You like my wiggle, don't you? Admit it? You can lay hands on me anytime." He grinned.

Tonya giggled and gave him a swat on the thigh.

"Stop it. Here she comes."

Kolby got out and opened Tonya's door, trying hard to remember how Grammie was related to Tonya's family. For him it was a jumble of names. Maybe she was a great aunt, or a distant cousin, no matter, she was a relation. Grammie and Willard attended every family event. Tonya distracted him from his thoughts when she bent over and got the deviled eggs and soy hot dogs out of the back seat. He leaned over her and whispered in her ear, "I truly appreciate the time you put in the gym."

"Shh."

He helped her out of the car, and smiled, then admired her cute butt. He shook his head as he watched Grammie all grizzled looking coming down the walk. What a stark contrast.

"Oh hello, Grammie," Tonya said. "It's so good to see you again. How's Willard?"

Kolby extended his arm to Grammie and assisted her up the flower lined sidewalk.

She pointed to the back yard, "Oh that old coot, he's fine. He's over there ogling at the girls dancing."

Tonya's parents' house was an ornate, stately Victorian painted pale yellow with black shutters. It had a large veranda lined with ferns and white wicker rocking chairs placed strategically. One side of the porch had a swing that held good memories for him and Tonya. They walked around to the large backyard that had a majestic and fragrant magnolia tree offering shade along with several mature pecan trees.

"Hi, Daddy." Tonya gave her dad a kiss and handed him the package of soy hot dogs.

"Girl, what is wrong with him? Who brings soy anything to a cookout?" he asked.

"Daddy, you keep forgetting he can't eat red meat. It makes him sick."

"That boy, he's way too delicate."

She rolled her eyes, gave him a brief hug then said, "Oh, Daddy, I know you like him."

"When I see who you could have married and you chose Kolby." Grinning, he shook his head in mock despair.

"Daddy, stop, I love him. Besides that's no way for a preacher to talk."

He grinned. "Baby girl, we do love him but some-times, listen"—he wiped the stream of perspiration from his face—"I know the Lord is no respecter of persons and Kolby is a believer. He is truly a good man. We are happy with him. He treats you good, and I can't ask for more." Her father glanced up from the burgers. "Uh oh, here comes your Uncle Steve, and you know his twisted feelings on interracial marriage. Steer clear of him. I'll handle him if he says anything ugly."

"Thanks, Daddy." She gave him a quick peck on the cheek while her dad turned back to the BBQ and Uncle Steve.

Kolby had to shuffle the food on the table around to find a spot for the deviled eggs among one of three tables filled with pies, mountains of beef ribs, chicken and hot dogs, potato salads, and such. It was a gastronomical event sure to make any stomach quake. Kolby set the eggs down then Kelvin asked Tonya and Kolby to dance the Electric Slide

She refused, but Kolby had to endure. It seems he was always the entertainment. He got up and purposely danced out of step, grinning sheepishly at Tonya and wiggled his hips.

Tonya buried her head when her mother said, "Tonya, what's wrong with him? Why is he wiggling like that?"

"Oh, Momma," Tonya said as she rolled her eyes at Kolby.

Her dad walked over. "Never mind, Portia, I will explain it to you later and do some wriggling of my own," was his sly reply.

Chapter 7

Angus answered his cell phone. "Hey, sister pants, what's up?"

"Nothing much, I haven't seen you in ages, and stop calling me that. Hey, I came across some old photos in Grandma and Grandpa's basement. You should come by and take a look at them. There's you and Brutus number three, Dad and you fishing and a horrid picture of me, Tonya, and Belissa in our PJs. Looks like we're about five and covered in calamine lotion. Someone wrote Poison Ivy on the back. I'm guessing it was Mom; looks like her handwriting. There's loads more."

"Sorry, I know it's been awhile. I've been picking up extra hours working security at school games and the mall. I'll be by later on. Do you want me to come by the house? There're few things I want to discuss with you.

"Like what?"

"Um, someone I am dating and see how Bryan is doing. Mom mentioned you're worried about him."

"He isn't doing well. We have been Skyping and arguing long distance about his drinking."

"Sorry to hear that. Hey, I just rounded the corner by your clinic. Can I swing by? I'll be quick. Are you busy now?"

"Nope. We don't have appointments until after lunch. Come on by. See you in a few," Clara said as she ended their call.

Riverside Veterinary Clinic was a few blocks from the town square in what was once an old gas station. His sister spent a lot of money refurbishing the place. The gas pump canopy was still there offering relief from the sun, wind and rain. The main area and waiting room were reserved for smaller pets. They'd renovated the ancient mechanic's shop in the back and turned it into an examination and treatment hospital for large animals—horses, cows, pigs and the like—with Macey's pet grooming covering almost the entire back of the property. The junkyard once littered with rusted out car bodies and truck carcasses, was clean and now an exercise area. It was a cute place. Several large wooden half-barrels filled with petunias lined each side of the path leading to the entrance. A huge plate-glass window decorated with silhouettes of a dog, a cat, and a bird advertised Riverside Veterinary Clinic in hefty block letters. Angus looked in and noticed Clara chatting on the phone as her assistant filed papers.

The door tinked with a bell sound as he walked in. The large waiting area had chairs and cushioned benches with dog and cat patterns lining the walls. A shelf of dog food stood in a corner advertising expensive organic, non-GMO, grain-free dog food most people in the town could not afford—each bag covered in dust.

The receptionist desk had the usual sign in sheet with a chained flowered pen and a canister of pet treats nearby. Behind the counter stood a floor-to-ceiling filing cabinet burgeoning with files and papers.

Clara removed her white lab coat and draped it over a chair to reveal her usual attire—jeans and T-shirt. She hung up the phone as she struggled to place a file in the cabinet and turned to greet Angus.

"Hey, big brother, I'm sure glad to see you. When can you pick up the photos?" She took a small sip of her soda and came around the corner to give Angus a quick hug.

"I'll pick them up today. Will that work? I need to wait until I finish my shift though. As soon as I get off work I'll head to your place. Should be there by 4:30. I also wanted to tell you to be on the lookout. There's been an uptick in drugs in the area, both prescription and street drugs."

"Don't I know it, that's why I am here taking a late lunch. The Ballard boys had their Labrador retriever, Willow, at the river, and it swam out to get what they thought was the white ball they'd thrown. The dog came back, dropped it on the ground, and started pawing it. Turns out it was a block of heroin. Did the family call you?"

"Yes. Sher and Mark are there now."

"The fentanyl in the heroin nearly killed the dog. I had to give her two rounds of Naloxone. I think she will recover, but it was a close."

"I hate to hear that. Everyone at the station is trying to figure out why the increase. We haven't seen much graffiti or gang dressing around. There's also been a significant rise in break-ins. Not sure why. I know Rex has an idea where it's coming from, but I can't discuss it."

"Did Mom invite you over for breakfast this weekend? With it being a holiday, the clinic is closed. I am hoping you will be able to make it."

"I'll be there, but I am bringing a guest."

"Who?"

"Belissa."

"Uh, who?" she asked as she raised an eyebrow and curled her lips in disgust. "Did you say Belissa?"

Leaning against the check in counter he said, "Uh huh."

"Belissa? What do you want with her? She's a mess. I call her Belissa of the three Bs."

"The what?"

"Belissa of the three Bs: Beauty, brains and boobs, plus she's a capital B."

"That's four Bs. And you're an adult. It's okay to say the big B word, no judging here."

"Funny how you can count but aren't concerned about the fourth B," Clara said. "Besides, I don't like cussing. It's a sign of a slow mind, poor vocabulary, and God doesn't care for it either. It's a lousy witness, it looks bad."

"She's not a B, she's high maintenance. So, you're worried God'll get you for saying the big B word but not about gossiping?"

"She's not the innocent girl we once knew. She's a badge bunny, you know the type always attracted to cops, a home wrecker. This isn't gossip. I know for a fact what happened, and I care about what happens to you. The officer you replaced left the force because of her. She drained him of his savings while he tried to hide the affair from his wife and kids. You need to steer clear of her. She's nothing but trouble. You have no idea what you're getting into with her."

"I'm a big boy, I can handle her. I got this." He snorted dismissively.

"Humph," Clara said as she picked up her purse and keys to leave. "I gotta go to the salon and get my hair styled, have a Mani-Pedi so I will look nice when I pick Bryan up at the joint base. I can't believe he is finally home."

"How long has it been? Fourteen months?" he asked.

"Nope, one year, four months, three days, and ten hours. He's been acting weird. He hasn't been calling me as much like he used to. I don't know what's going on with him. I'm concerned. All we do is argue. I want to create a small man-cave in the basement. It's the perfect place. He'll need somewhere to unwind given all he has seen on this last tour of duty. I need you to pick up a newly reupholstered sofa at the thrift store and a small bar sized fridge. I want to make it nice for him as soon as I can. Can you come by this weekend and help me while he's getting settled in?"

"Sure, I can help, glad to."

Clara smiled. "You'll be by early tomorrow to help with the celebration BBQ, right?"

"I'll be there," he groused, not relishing the idea of the dog slobbers and having to navigate and pick up the yard bombs when it came time for the outside work.

"Okay, see you soon. You can get the sofa then?"

"Yah, Kolby and I'll be there."

"Pick up Tonya and bring her with you please. She can help me with the BBQ setup. We should have plenty of time. Bryan gets in about ten tonight, and the cookout is tomorrow afternoon."

"See you, sis." He left and then resumed his cruising around town.

He decided to go to the Guiliani City Park, named after a much loved and missed officer who passed away a few years back who had dedicated his life to the youth of the town and the Police Athletic League. He chatted with some kids, tossed a football with them, showing them a few of his moves from his high school days, and when he heard the ice cream truck, he bought rocket popsicles for each of them. He threw a long pass with the football to one of the boys and walked back to the squad car when the delicious aroma from the Terrific Taco food truck hit him. It was lunch time, so he ordered the colossal taco special.

"Man, you guys have *the* best tacos," he said biting into it. Mid-bite he got a call on the shoulder radio.

"Angus, you have a 10-60, lockout at your place." Jean said.

"Let me guess, Grammie again? That's the third time she's locked herself out since I've been back." He growled in frustration. "You know she can quote Scripture all day long but remember to *not* lock herself out of the house, nope. Be there in a few, I'm leaving the park now."

Grammie and Willard were in a heated argument on the well-manicured front lawn. Her arms waved wildly about in the air, pointing her knobby fingers at Willard. She was wearing a loud pink and blue floral robe, had curlers in her hair, and the obligatory stretch wristwatch with tissues tucked in the metal elastic band. Willard stood tall, patting his well-groomed mustache and looking irritated at the same time. His brown pants hung loosely at his legs—suspenders and wrinkled front pocket plaid leisure shirt, Sans shoes completed his outfit.

"Oh, Angus, I sure am glad you're here," Grammie said. "Houdini, our Tuxedo cat, got loose again. We went after him, but then we got locked out."

"I know, Grammie, that's why I'm here."

"Well," Willard said, "he seems to be hiding in the hedge bushes along the side door. He won't come out. Can't figure out why. I told Erma here to get the keys before going outside, but no, she didn't see the keys on the table because she lost her glasses again!" he said throwing his hands up and rolling his eyes. "I swear she'd lose her head if it wasn't attached."

"Oh, stop your grumbling, Willard. I declare all you ever do is complain, now shut your face."

Willard mumbled under his breath.

Angus chuckled and remembered the nickname he and Clara had for them—the Bickersons. He fished around in his pocket for the keys Grammie had given him in the event of an emergency when he moved into the garage.

"Guess I need to trim the grass," Angus muttered and walked across the yard to the front door. "I know what I'll be doing tonight."

He walked over to the screened-in door and noticed it wasn't locked!

When he opened the door, Willard shouted, "Hallelujah, now I can finish the game," and rushed past Angus.

Grammie was still at the bushes. Bending over, she said in a warbly voice, "Houdini, Houdini, come on out, you dern ole cat. I can't figure out why he isn't coming," she said as she slowly stood clutching her back.

Angus walked over to the shrubs, peered in, and caught sight of something black and white, but it wasn't a cat. "Skunk!" Angus hollered then beat a path away from the animal. He thought he'd cleared the path, but tripped over the buckled sidewalk, going head first into the lawn getting grass stains all over his shirt. Too late, he looked up and saw a pair of wrinkly brown legs with worn slippers the size of barges run past him. He lifted his head and realized he was looking straight into the back end of the skunk. In vain, he tried to shield himself from the inevitable spray, it was no use; he was directly in the line of fire.

Coughing and gagging, he curled up in a fetal position in agony, tears running down his face, gasping for breath as the pungent odor assaulted his nostrils and lungs. He struggled, unable to get to his feet, noting that for a decrepit old lady, Grammie sure managed to get out of the way quickly. He rolled on the grass and looked at Willard doubled over slapping his thighs, laughing and wiping away tears. Apparently, the skunk was only intent on marking him, and then it ran into the woods behind the house as Grammie sprinted past Angus while Willard held the door open for her.

Angus staggered, wiped his burning eyes on his shirt sleeve and flew up the steps to his place, all the while cussing and stripping off his uniform. Holding his breath, he placed the offensive smelling clothes in the washer, using the hottest setting and extra-strength detergent. He could only hope they weren't ruined.

Trying to inhale as little as possible, he walked to the kitchen, grabbed the vinegar, and then got the hydrogen peroxide from the medicine cabinet and stepped into the shower. He scrubbed for ages, but still smelled of skunk when he got out. He dressed in an old pair of jeans and a T-shirt and returned to the squad car.

He radioed in. "Jean, its Angus. Listen, I've been sprayed by a skunk. Geez, I don't think I'll ever get rid of the smell. I don't think y'all will want to be around me today. Let Rex know, will you? I'll shower and scrub a few more times. Maybe by tomorrow y'all will be able tolerate me being there. Hey, can you send Sher or Mark over to get the squad car please? I'd appreciate it."

"Sure thing, Angus, I'll tell Rex. See ya then."

"Thanks, Jean."

Angus leaned back against the car seat and groaned knowing he'd have to face all kinds of jokes and comments like, hey Pepe Le Pew, you're a real stinker or something else even more hokey when he returned to work. Since his shift was almost over, he went back into the apartment to get his Bronco keys and head over to his sister's, then to the thrift store to pick up the sofa.

He pulled into Clara's driveway, got out and walked across the wood deck, and opened the back door. An odor far worse than skunk attacked his nose. He gagged and tucked his nose into the front of his shirt. Clara sat crying, pushing back her hair and scrubbing the wooden floor.

"Good god, Clara, what is that awful stench?" he exclaimed.

"Oh, remember the lovely robotic vacuum you bought me last year for Christmas? Well, Brutus and Bullet got sick. They pooped and puked, then the vacuum smeared it all over the house. They ran through it while chasing the vacuum. I just got back from the salon, had my nails and hair done, and put on the sexy shirt I bought at the mall to greet Bryan in, and I come home to this!" She threw her hands up in the air, "I give up, I'll never get this cleaned in time." In an attempt to clean she wiped the floor, smearing another glob of puke.

Angus surveyed the area. Piles of paper towels were scattered throughout the room. Three empty tubes of paper towels lay by the leather sofa. Streaks of poop ran under the coffee table, which led to the end tables, which led to under the sofa, and came out by the floor lamp and around the brick fireplace. *What an enormous mess.*

Clara started sobbing and laughing maniacally at the same time. Angus chuckled at her, which only made her cry more. He helped her up and took her into the kitchen and sat her down at the table. He noticed a trail of poop-puke under the cabinets and said, "Holy crap, it's everywhere."

"Eww, Angus you stink like a skunk," she said pinching her nose.

"I know, it's a long embarrassing story," he sighed and took out his cell to call her friend.

"Hey, Tonya, it's Angus. Can you swing by and get Clara? Bullet and Brutus made an enormous mess, and now she's a mess. Can you take her back to the salon? You can? That's great, thanks. Oh, and before I forget, tell Kolby to not bother coming over. Thanks," he said ending the call. He would have to help with the man cave another day.

Clara clasped her hands and begged, "Can you take the dogs to Macey's? She can clean them real quick, please?"

"Ah, man, I really don't want to go there." But the mournful pout on his sister's face and her continued begging told him he had no choice.

"Come on, you stinky beasts," he said while herding the smelly dogs.

"The leashes are by the back door," Clara said. "Thank you so much, Angus. I truly appreciate your helping me."

"Yeah, yeah," he said and clipped the leashes on the dogs.

He loaded the dogs into his old Bronco and took them over to Macey's Pawsome Pet Grooming place. He really didn't want to see her. He was certain it would be uncomfortable. His only other alternative was to bathe the brutes himself, and that wasn't happening.

He pulled around back. Clara must have called her right away as Macey was at the door. He got the two beasts out of his Bronco, crying to himself when he realized how hard it was going to be to get the skunk *and* the dog odors out.

"Hello, Macey," he said as the dogs pulled him in the door. She stood there with her back to him tying a black plastic apron around her small waist, and reached for the dog shampoo and gloves.

"Hello, Angus," she said, her back to him.

The dogs, recognizing her voice, became excited, farted, and ran to her, at the same time.

"Well hello, Brutus and Bullet. My, don't you two stink," she said and patted each one saying their names in quiet tones to calm them down.

Other than the first time he saw her on the bridge, she hadn't changed much. She still had the long black hair, a great figure and beautiful smile. For a split second, his heart softened, and making the most of the moment he said, "You know, I truly am sorry. I didn't know—"

She cut him off before he could finish. Looking down at her feet she said, "It's okay," and took the dogs to the back, as Angus quietly let himself out.

He got in the Bronco, and picked up his phone. "Mom, can you meet me at Clara's? The dogs got sick all over, and it's a real disaster. I gotta get it cleaned before Bryan gets home tonight."

"Sure, honey, be right there," his mom answered.

"Thanks, Mom." He hung up the phone, glad to have the help. There's no way he was going to clean the mess up by himself.

Chapter 8

*The Lord is not slow in keeping his promise,
as some understand slowness. Instead he is patient with you,
not wanting anyone to perish,
but everyone to come to repentance.*
2 Peter 3:9 (NIV)

It had been a few days since the skunk debacle. The sun was shining, and Angus decided to go by the cleaners to pick up his sanitized, deodorized, and five times laundered uniform on the way to the family breakfast. The BBQ had been cancelled so Clara and Bryan could have some much needed alone time.

"What a beautiful day," Angus said out loud to no one in particular. He drove past his place and watched Grammie hanging sheets on the line while Houdini cleaned himself and watched from a window. Further down the road, people were out in the early morning sun planting shrubs, walking their dogs, or chatting with the neighbors. He smiled when he realized he had come to appreciate small-town life.

He pulled into the parking lot of Joey's BBQ. Looking up, he gawked at the brand new advertisement emblazoned on the side of the brick building—"Joey's BBQ-bar and grille" with a big stack of ribs emblazoned with the words "You Don't Need Teeth to Eat Our Beef. We Deliver." The phone number was followed by Eat Beef beneath the ribs.

He considered honking but remembered the manners his dad taught him: always go to the door for your date *and* open the car door. This was their sixth date, and he was hoping it would be a "stay the night date."

He knocked on the door. Belissa hollered, "If that's you, Angus, come on in. I am almost ready. If it's you Joey, I ain't workin' an extra shift today. Go away!"

Angus glanced around the room. He wasn't sure what he expected, maybe something girly, but he had to admit as hardened as he was, even he was taken aback when he laid his eyes on two books, about witchcraft, spells and the occult on the coffee table. *How odd there's a Bible right next to the books. Talk about a conflict.* On the lumpy sofa were several occult magazines about séances, astrology, palm reading and sorcery.

In spite of the room's many windows, it had a gloomy and depressing atmosphere. She had decorated the walls with various ankhs, and weird pentagrams with half-moons on each side of the ankhs. He was rethinking the whole stay the night date thing. He was no prude, but the occult made him uneasy. He had heard stories and seen enough in his line of duty to believe there really was a devil even though he wouldn't admit it to anyone.

Belissa came out of the bathroom wearing black tights, high-heeled steam punk-style buckled black knee-high boots, and a long sleeve deep burgundy top barely covering her smooth stomach. He gazed at her taunt stomach and smiled. He was glad she wore long sleeves; he wasn't sure how his folks would react to her sleeve tattoos of red-eyed goats, upside down crosses, and a black pentagram.

Her makeup was expertly applied—dark eyeliner, smoky eyes, contoured cheeks. Her long hair fell on her shoulders, and wisps of bangs complimented her face.

"Hey, I'm ready. Let's go, before Joey comes up here again. I'm starving, and your mom's breakfast sounds good. I hope she is making her scrumpdillyicious biscuits and gravy."

"As far as I know, she is," Angus said opening the door for her.

She locked the door, and they walked quietly down the steps to his Bronco. Neither wanted to talk, so most of the ride to his folks' house was silent. He was wondering how his mom and dad would respond to Belissa, and hoped neither would get preachy.

She turned towards him. "I'm guessing Clara and Macey will be there."

"Probably."

"Okay, but it might get uncomfortable. We've haven't spoken since middle school."

"Guess I didn't notice, too busy with sports." He came to a stop and looked both ways. "Why'd you quit being friends?"

"They told my mom I was into séances, Tarot cards, Ouija board, and said I was casting spells." She rolled her eyes.

"I remember hearing something about that. Were you?"

"I did one séance but I never cast spells. I told kids that when they'd do something to tick me off."

"With their backward beliefs it's not surprising. Church people, go figure." He turned the radio down.

"I got grounded and a huge lecture from the youth pastor." She snorted loudly.

"Sorry, I thought it had something to do with your folks' divorce, but that doesn't make sense. My folks always tried to keep adult stuff a secret from us. They'd say, 'It's grown up talk.'"

"What happened with him?"

She turned and continued looking out the window. "My dad came home one day saying he didn't love my mom, said he never did, and that he's leaving. He whips out pictures of his new love, like he's proud of her." She wiped away a tear. "Then he walked out the kitchen door, got into his new convertible Corvette. Haven't seen him since."

Angus stopped the vehicle, rubbed her shoulder, and in a soothing tone asked, "Wow, I'm sorry. You okay?"

"Yah. I don't want to talk about it anymore." She sighed.

He drove on and pulled the Bronco into his parents' driveway, and noticed Clara and Bryan had already arrived at the house. Getting out to open the door for Belissa, he saw Kolby and Tonya pull up in a shiny new minivan. *That's odd, a minivan?* He turned and saw his mom had planted dahlias, and the autumn crocuses emerged through the grass and were budding.

"Belissa, it is so good to see you," his mom said and gave her a quick hug. "It's been a long time. How are you? How's your mom today? I caught a glimpse of her at church last week, and she didn't look well."

"Oh, I didn't know she was sick. I haven't seen her a week or so."

His mom walked over to Kolby's car and gave him a big hug and beamed when Tonya got out of the car. "How are you doing, Tonya? Are you tired? Sick? I know you must be hungry! Especially with two in the oven!"

Angus stopped mid stride with his mouth hanging open and said, "Did I hear that right? Twins?"

"Yes," Kolby said grinning, "Tonya is pregnant with twins!"

"Twins! Dude, you've been married five years and nothing, I assumed you were shooting blanks all these years. I'd say with twins you're off to a good start. Congratulations, bud," he said and slapped Kolby on the back.

"Okay, everyone, let's go inside. I have the biscuits and gravy ready," his mom said.

"Mom, rumor has it you've been suffering from allergies. That's what Dad said when I saw him at the hardware store. So, I brought some canned biscuits in case you weren't up to baking a big batch of fresh biscuits," Angus said as they all walked to the back door.

"Canned biscuits! Boy, what's wrong with you? You know better. Have I ever made canned biscuits? This is the South. We don't do canned biscuits," his mom said with a smile as she swatted his arm.

"Good, I was hoping you'd say that," he said and gave her a quick hug. He glanced around, spotting Macey.

A smile flashed across his face, and his heart pounded. She still had the same effect on him. For a flickering moment all was well with the world, until Clara, Tonya, and Macey saw Belissa walk in.

Anne held her breath; uncertain as to how this would pan out. The girls smiled politely and acknowledged Belissa.

"Hello, Belissa," they said flatly in unison.

"Hello," Belissa said smiling. She turned and sat next to Bryan at the dining room table.

The three girls sat and talked in their *Gilmore Girls* style with Macey frequently saying words in her quirky, individualistic way.

"Hey, there's a new sexy perfume we could get for Angie's bridal shower." Macey pronounced perfume as if it had three syllables.

Angus overheard the three talking and stole a glance at her and smiled. *She always mispronounced certain words like lingerie, it became ling-er-ee. Stop, there's no going back. She'd never forgive me.*

Before she could finish, Tonya added, "Oh, she'd like that."

Clara blurted out, "Let's have the shower at the lyceum in the library."

"Hey, we can decorate it with fresh flowers, and toile, and get some antiques for photo shots, and serve champagne, and giggle as we go through all the lingerie she will get!" Macey said trying to talk over Clara excitedly.

"Oh, I can't stand the wait," Tonya said.

Belissa caught Angus looking at Macey and promptly got up from the table, sauntered over and put her arms around his waist and gave him a long, big kiss, in front of everyone. Macey put on a brave face and turned away as Tonya and Clara closed ranks around her.

"Time to eat, Will!" his mom hollered. When he didn't respond, she asked Angus, "Get your father from the den. He's in there watching sports on ESPN. Tell him it's time for him to say grace and for us to sing our song."

"All right, I heard you," his dad hollered. Honestly, Anne? Must we sing *Deep in the Heart of Texas* before every family gathering?"

"Why, yes, we do, Will. Now don't argue. Say grace and let's sing so we can get to eating."

Everyone except Belissa bowed their heads, afterwards they started singing the song.

"The stars at night are big and bright, boom, boom, boom, boom, deep in the heart of Texas. The prairie sky is wide and high, boom, boom, boom, boom, deep in the heart of Texas." They all continued singing as Angus and his dad stomped their boots to each boom. Once they finished singing, they sat and began passing the biscuits and gravy, scrambled eggs, sausage, and of course grits.

"Mom, I gotta say, you haven't lost your touch," Angus said piling more gravy on his plate.

"Sure hasn't," his dad said rubbing his belly. "Best cook in this here town."

"Oh, contraire, Dad, I'd say county."

Anne smiled and passed the sausage gravy to Belissa.

"I sure am glad to be back and have some real grits and homemade sausage and gravy," Angus said. "It doesn't taste as good up North."

After everyone had eaten their fill, Anne cleared the table. Dishes and utensils clanked in the sink as the three girls chatted about the twins while washing and wiping the dishes.

Angus sensed Belissa felt awkward and decided now would be a good time to leave, until he spotted a lone biscuit on the counter looking forlorn and needing to be eaten. His dad also saw the biscuit and made a lunge for it at the exact same time as Angus.

"Not so fast, old man. Ha! Got it first!" he exclaimed. In order to fend off his dad, he ran into the living room. Brutus also wanted the biscuit and jumped trying to get it from Angus who exclaimed, "It's mine, you brute! Get back!"

"Not so fast, big guy." Will, as swift and agile as a gazelle, leapt onto the coffee table and grabbed the biscuit from Angus who had lifted it in the air to prevent Brutus from inhaling it without taking the time to savor its delicious flakiness.

"Hah! It's mine," his dad said shoving the biscuit in his mouth with a look of triumph as the crowd from the kitchen cheered him on.

They stared at each other. Angus stood, his mouth agape with an expression of shock on his face. As his dad, with a triumphant gleam, finished shoving the biscuit into his mouth.

"Oh, boys, lookie here!" Anne said as she held up a warm zip lock bag of leftover biscuits, gently dangling them in the air.

Will fell to the carpet grabbing his ankle and winced.

"Faker! Nice try, old man. Not gonna work this time, at least not when there're homemade biscuits at stake," Angus said grinning and rushed to grab the biscuits.

His dad stood, shrugged his shoulders and said, "Hey, it was worth a try."

Angus reverted back to his glory days when he was a high school quarterback. He turned, and passed a quick Hail Mary, tossing the bag of still warm biscuits to Belissa. It was close, but she caught the bag as he grabbed the leftover sausage gravy in the used butter tub on the counter, and they ran out the door laughing as Will shouted, "No! Anne, those were mine!"

Angus chuckled and held the door for Belissa. He started the car and maneuvered around Kolby's car in the extra wide driveway.

Inside the car, Belissa asked, "I forgot, why do y'all sing *Deep in the Heart of Texas* at every family get together?"

Angus looked both ways then pulled out of the drive and said, "Years ago we moved here for work reasons, and my mom being a Texan, swore she'd never forget Texas. I guess it's her way of staying true to her roots."

"I enjoyed being with your folks today. They're so nice and caring. I always had the best time at your house growing up."

"What? My parents? Nice? Caring? I thought you'd be uncomfortable around them."

"Why would you think that? You have no idea how good you have it." She popped a CD into the car's dash.

Instead of heading to her place, they decided to go to the car show the next county over. Angus wondered to himself if this would be like all their other dates—starts out good but ends with her being upset. Once, while she was in the ladies room, she became upset when he took a few bites of her fries without asking. In a low voice she leaned across the table and asked him, "Are you concerned about my weight? Am I fat? Is that why you're eating my food?" Completely blowing his social faux pas out of proportion, you'd have thought he took the last morsel of food from a hungry child. She warned him the next time they went out to eat.

"Hey, let's go to the auto show. How's that sound?"

"Sure, I guess."

"Don't sound so enthused."

She rolled down the car's window, not bothering to reply.

He got on the highway and drove to the next town over. *Well, she looks like she's in a great mood.* The parking lot was crowded, and he had to wedge the Bronco into the last spot. It was a tight fit. They walked across the gravel parking lot.

"Ouch." She stumbled. "I wish I'd of known we'd be doing all this walking."

"Here." He held her hand to steady her walk.

He paid the attendant $10 for parking, as they continued on in silence holding hands, pausing long enough to navigate around the mud puddles from the recent rain.

It was a rare warm autumn day. The sun was out, and the fall violas in purple and white planted near the entrance filled the air with their sweet fragrance.

Once inside the complex, they stopped to view the cars and marvel at the immense monster trucks. He took a quick selfie at an antique Cadillac and said, "Next I want to look at that classic red Corvette in the next row."

Irritated, Belissa folded her arms across her chest, tapped her foot and said, "Angus, honey, I'm bored. Can we go? I've seen enough of these old cars."

"I was patient when you wanted to look at your pink and purple roadsters."

"But I want to go, now," she whined. *All these stupid cars. He wasn't paying attention when I told him my dad drove off in a Corvette. I have to get outta here.* She stroked Angus arm and said, "Please Angus, let's go."

He rolled his eyes. "We just got here." His thoughts trailed off to more pleasant relationships.

She caught him smiling and asked, "What're you smiling about?"

He gritted his teeth and said, "Uh, nothing."

She blurted out, "You're thinking of someone else, another woman, aren't you? I can tell from your stupid grin. Don't deny it." She pouted.

He rubbed his temples and sighed. "I'm not." Then muttered, "Here we go again."

"I promise it will be worth your while, if we leave now," she said as she pulled him close.

He grinned, wrapped his arms around her waist and gave her a small kiss.

"Oh, you can do better. You can show me later on," she said pressing her body into his.

He was conflicted, his heart wanted Macey but his body had very different thoughts. Trying to distract himself and give his mind a chance to return to his "normal" guy thoughts he said, "Hey, let's get something to eat."

"Eat?" Her eyes widened at the thought. "I have to watch my figure."

Though full from breakfast, he ate funnel cake, fried Oreos, and fried Snickers, and polished it off with a draft beer. His mind returned to Macey—she would enjoy the unique foods, only she'd have said u-knee-q foods.

"You like my figure don't you? Want to see more of it, naked?" she said as she pressed her body into his and ran her fingers on his bicep.

Distracting him from his thoughts, she whispered to him, "I promise you'll love what I have planned."

"Sure, let's go."

Evening came quick, and about eight they headed back to Riverside. It was a cool evening, and they sat in the car chatting. Angus angled in closer to her and tried to run his fingers through her hair, but she pulled away, complaining it took her a long time to style and didn't want it messed up for work the next day. He readjusted and after much kissing, Belissa invited Angus up to her place. He sat there wanting to go up, but he had a nagging feeling he shouldn't accept her invitation. Angus decided to go home, he had to work the next day, and he knew if he stayed the night, he would not get much sleep.

"As much as I hate to say it, I don't think I can." *What am I nuts?* His body wanted her, but he didn't want to deal with her whining. Before he could change his mind, and he truly wanted too, she became mad.

***

Belissa was not only disappointed, she was angry. Not waiting for him to open the car door for her, she flung it open and shut it so hard the whole car shook. She stomped up the steps, swearing the whole way, jammed the keys into the lock, and slammed the door behind her.

Belissa was not accustomed to being turned down. His rejection caused a searing pain in her heart reminding her of her father. *You can't do to me what he did. I am in control not you, Angus. Leaving me alone, after what I offered!*

The only thing she hated more than rejection was being alone, especially at night. She flicked on all the lights in her place, threw her keys on the kitchen counter, and despite not being hungry, she grabbed the praline ice cream from the freezer and ate a gigantic spoonful, wincing as brain freeze set in causing tears to well up. Tossing the spoon into the sink, she dragged herself to the worn and lumpy sofa and collapsed.

She turned on the TV—some insipid rerun of *Touched by an Angel* was on the air. Hmmpf, *Touched by an Angel,* what garbage. She stared blankly at the TV for a few moments knowing what was coming next. The same old persistent show replayed in her mind. Memories of when and how her dad left them, the weight gain in high school, how girls teased her and she would retaliate by beating them up. Almost anything set her off: a supposed angry look, a whisper, and if in a particularly bad mood, even a smile. In her hurt, she retaliated by beating the offender without mercy.

While at a friend's house she discovered the occult. During a séance, Belissa called forth a teen who had died in a car wreck earlier that year. To everyone's astonishment the teen answered. From then on, Belissa became the school expert on all things occult. Whether it was Tarot card reading, pyramid power, divination, astrology or casting spells, she relished the power the occult gave and the fear it invoked in others.

She knew she was unhappy, but felt powerless to make any changes. The accumulation of past troubles created deep layers of anguish with endless ruts of sorrow. The hurts squeezed the very life from her wounded soul. She heard the demons whisper as they danced, forming a conga line of lies telling her to "Just end it now. No one loves you. You don't deserve love. Your own father didn't want you. You still have those pain pills."

Belissa stared at the tattered old Bible on the coffee table; it had been in the family for generations. She couldn't bring herself to deface it or throw it out, so she kept it nearby as a source of unexplained comfort. She opened and shut it several times, trying to read it through her tears, but after a few moments closed it, unable to concentrate.

She grabbed a tissue, hugged a pillow and then cried herself to sleep on the shabby, stained sofa. She was in a deep tormented dream, and didn't hear her cell phone ring.

Angus ended the call not bothering to leave a voicemail. *Guess she's pretty mad.* She didn't hear the call and she certainly didn't hear Christ calling her, weeping over her as she continued to push away his gift of love.

Chapter 9

*Let them drink and forget their poverty
and remember their misery no more.
Proverbs 31:7 (NIV)*

Clara and Bryan had spent the last few days arguing, specifically over his drinking. He had been back five weeks and had been to the liquor store four times and had gone through three bottles of whiskey and four cases of beer. He had been at the bar on several occassions, coming home falling down drunk three of those times. Bryan was not handling transitioning from military life as a medic to a nurse at Mercy Hospital well. Clara was unhappy and unsure how to help him.

"Bryan, aren't you going to church?" The arguing started early. "It could help with what you're dealing with."

"Nah, don't feel like it today." He stretched and poked his head in the fridge. "I don't think I can. I used to go when I was a kid, back when all the world was bright and sunny. It ain't that kinda world anymore. Now where is that last beer? I need a little hair of the dog that bit me," he said as he searched for another beer.

"Really? It's 10:00 a.m. on a Sunday. And you're already drinking? Honestly, I don't know if I can do this."

"What of it? Who cares if it's Sunday or not? I've lost hope. You'd be that way too if you've seen what I've seen," he said popping the top off of another beer. Musing aloud, he said, "Gonna have to make another beer run. I'm low on supplies," he said loud enough for her to hear.

"I don't know what is going on. You aren't the same since you came back," she said with a lump in her throat. "I understand you've lost hope. I get it. But drinking isn't the answer."

"Ya think? How's about you hope for the both of us? I can't. Right now, I'm hoping there's another beer in the garage fridge," he said derisively, peering over the top of the beer can.

"Your sarcasm doesn't help. I am trying my best to understand why you are drinking so much."

"Hmm, let me see. Could it be that I have seen the insides of the human body, young, old, civilian, and military in ways you'll never see and I can't unsee?"

She reached for his hands. "Tell me about what happened."

He flinched and jerked his hand away. "I can't. I don't want to tell you, you'd never understand. I want to forget the things I saw, but my mind keeps playing the scenes. It's like a never ending television horror movie. It keeps rebroadcasting, rewinding, it doesn't stop. That's why I drink. It's why most of the guys drink."

He pulled out a wooden chair and straddled it. "On top of that, I come home, and you're the big boss, telling me what I need to do, where I need to go, when to go to work, or church. Nagging me and telling me I drink too much. You think I don't know that? You think I like being told what to do? I'm a grown-ass man. You better get used to this. I'm not changing. This is how I deal with stress now. It's my go to."

"Well, Bryan, it isn't my go to. I can't take this. It's been weeks. You barely talk to me or touch me. You go to work, come home, sit in front of the TV, and drink all night. If this is what our marriage is going to be, I won't be around long."

"Is that a threat?" Bryan belched.

"No." She blew her nose and said defiantly, "It's a promise."

"Ain't that against our vows?"

"It is, but I can't do this. You aren't the same person. You don't even try anymore."

"Try? What's to try? Just as I am, baby." He got up and leaned against the counter and held his can of beer high in the air as if to toast her. "For better or for worse."

"I need to get away for a while. Angry talk isn't getting us anywhere. I am going to Mom and Dad's." She got the dogs, patted down her pockets then dug through her purse. "Where are the keys to the truck?"

He threw the keys on the counter at her. "Here they are."

She gave him a disgusted look and slammed the door behind her.

But not before Bryan hollered, "That's right, run to Mommy and Daddy. I'm sure they'll side with you!" He scratched his belly, walked to the fridge, and got another cold one and plopped in front of the TV to watch reruns of *Jackass*.

The TV and beer momentarily took his mind off of the memories in Afghanistan. Without wanting to, he recalled the bodies, mangled limbs, blood squirting, men moaning, women and small children dying on the table. And the terrorists and combatants trying to fight the medical team even as they were trying to save their wretched lives.

He recalled one particular terrorist covered in blood screaming at the top of his voice, "Allah Akbar," Bryan let him wait in *triage,* labeling his injuries yellow, and making him wait for medical attention. He should have worked on him, saved him, but he let him die a slow, agonizing death. Bit by bit the screams dissipated, and then all went quiet. Now his conscience bothered him. He knew what he did was unethical, morally wrong, and he caught hell from the FST—Forward Surgical Team— and his commanding officer. There was an investigation, his file was flagged, and after a psychiatric evaluation they determined he had severe PTSD. With little improvement shown, the mandatory counseling ended, and the Army sent him home.

Overcome with guilt and confusion he rubbed his stomach. "Geez am I getting an ulcer?"

As a medic he had to treat the enemy, but treating an enemy combatant was another story. Why did he feel guilty about letting him die when the combatant was hell bent on killing him and any other American soldier he found? Why the guilt? Fingers of panic and anxiety worked their way up his body starting at his toes, causing them to curl. Like a snake, the unwelcome emotions slithered up his legs, finally working its stranglehold up to his chest. He took another chug, grateful for its temporary relief.

He stared at the beer can, a blank look on his face. Then he peered into it hoping to find a magical elixir to help him forget. Drinking wasn't helping; the alcohol no longer erased the gory memories. Attending church didn't help much, and it didn't seem the same. In his mind he could not reconcile the war, the hate, and the carnage. Not any of it.

Leaving the kitchen, he hiccupped and pounded the wall asking, "Why, God? I don't understand. Why did they have to die?" he yelled at the ceiling in anguish.

He walked to the window, and pulled back the curtains. Numb, he stared outside. His mind took him back to the FST hospital tent, seeing his buddies being rushed in on gurneys, IVs attached and covered in blood, laid out on the table, blood trails on the floor, spurting on the walls like a twisted abstract painting, blood on the scrubs, bloody plasma bags and needles. Blood, everywhere. The screams and moans repeated like a warped record. He could never forget their cries as they replayed in his mind.

The team tried to save them all, but it was no use. Soldiers with detached limbs, barely alive by the time they reached them, but still the FST nurses and doctors worked expertly and frantically, sometimes able to work miracles and save them, though not always with the same number of body parts they came in with. He remembered collecting dog tags, wiping them clean, and making preparations for the removal of the bodies. He grew tired of seeing it over and over again daily, hourly in microscopic and vivid detail.

God didn't answer his questions at least not right away, but in the silence, Bryan thought back to a sermon Pastor Andrews, Tonya's dad, gave on love and forgiveness. Pastor's words to love your enemies and pray for them stuck in his throat.

He could see Pastor at the podium in jeans and suit jacket, animatedly pointing his finger at the congregation, pacing back and forth, trying to get them to realize all Christ did for each of them, for *all,* including your enemies, including the unlovable.

"Christ was willing that none should perish. Love is a small word, only four letters, but it's a big word, an impacting word, a life-changing word," he preached.

"Love carries the weight of the world. Love came to earth, love saved you and them. Love that waits for all to come to him, love conquers their hate, love conquers your hate. Love your enemies."

He paused at the podium and looked out at the congregation, saying, "John chapter 13 shows us how Christ loved an enemy, a sinner. Most people miss this in the foot washing narrative, but Christ washed Judas' feet knowing he was the one who would betray him. It may startle you to hear this, but I believe Christ loved and prayed for him to turn from his evil task. Despite knowing his betrayal, he washed Judas' feet—Judas an enemy of the Gospel."

Pastor took off his eyeglasses, stepped onto the main floor area and continued. "Christ showed love and compassion towards Judas. I know that sounds impossible, difficult at best. Remember Christ loves us all, even while we were yet sinners. Love and forgiveness are the essence of God's nature and we are to be imitators of him. His love brings you peace if you will ask. His perfect *love* casts out all fear, all anxiety."

Bryan jerked the curtains shut nearly pulling down the rods and yelled, "Love your enemies? You got to be kidding. That's not possible!"

He heard a calm, peaceful whisper, "Yes, Bryan, it is. I loved those who beat me, whipped me, and nailed me to a cross. Forgiveness, Bryan. Let me love you. Abide in my love, and you will learn to forgive so you can experience lasting peace."

He hung his head, and for the first time since leaving Afghanistan, he wept. Waves of calm and serenity, washed over him cleansing him, calming him, and he felt the anxiety leave him. Deep mournful guttural sobs rose from his belly and crept up his throat and wailed out of his mouth. He cried for his lost friends, he cried for his buddies who died on the battle field, the grieving families, and he cried for himself. In the depths of this refining, he collapsed on the sofa and slept in peace.

***

Clara took the dogs for a walk to clear her head then drove through town. She stopped at the local coffee shop, grabbed a latte, and headed to her folks' house, glad to see their cars in the driveway.

Brutus and Bullet ran in as she opened the screen door. "Mom, Dad, where are you?" She walked to the living room. Her dad glanced up and lowered the TV's volume.

"What's wrong honey? You look like you've been crying."

"Oh, Mom, it's Bryan. All we ever do is argue." She sniffled. "I don't think I can take his drinking anymore."

"Here, sweetie, have a seat. Will hand me the tissue please."

Clara put her purse on the end table and flopped on the sofa. "All he does is drink. He goes to the bar and the liquor store sometimes twice a week. He's even missed work. I'm afraid he's going to lose his job. I hate being home and I don't want to go back."

"Clara, honey, I know you don't want to go back, but you have to. Marriage is tough. Bryan is smart. He'll pull out of this," her mom said as she stroked Clara's hair, hugging her closely.

"Baby girl, God will see you through. Bryan knows what he's doing is wrong, he knows drinking won't fix anything, and he has God's Word hidden in his heart. The Bible says he remains faithful even when we aren't."

"I know, Mom. He's been so mean-spirited, saying awful things. It hurts. It really hurts."

"I know, sweetie, I truly do, but you need to go back and be with him," her mom said.

"You're right. Please pray he'll change soon. I don't know how much more of his drinking I can take," Clara said as she blew her nose.

"Come on, Brutus and Bullet, let's go." The dogs stretched and whined but were obedient as Clara left.

Taking her time, she headed home and parked the car in the driveway. Gripping the steering wheel, she rested her head against it, praying for the strength to overcome her reluctance to go inside.

She opened the door as the dogs bounded in. She quietly laid the keys on the kitchen counter and noticed Bryan in the living room asleep. She wasn't sure if she should wake him, or let him sleep. If she woke him another round of arguing could start, and all the quarreling wore her out.

The sofa gently sighed when she sat next to him. She brushed the sweaty hair from his face. He looked a wreck, sleeping there wearing a beer-stained holey T-shirt. His eyes were red and swollen, and yet he looked like a child at peace.

Deciding to let him sleep, she whispered to the dogs, "No, down," and stopped them before they jumped on the sofa.

Bryan rolled over and groaned and sat up when Clara gently brushed a lock of thick blond hair from his brow. He stirred and held his head in his hands as the dogs leapt on him.

"Hey there, buddies." He smiled and laughed as Brutus and Bullet licked him, their tails wagging violently.

Clara hadn't heard him laugh since he'd been back. She sat on the couch next to him and he pulled her close.

"Look, I'm sorry. Let's not talk about the big 'D' and don't leave me. We vowed to never divorce. I'll do whatever you want."

Clara wasn't sure if she should believe him.

She bit her lip and said, "Okay, let's check into some PTSD treatment for you at the VA hospital, or perhaps Christian counseling. I think Tonya's dad, Pastor Andrews, can recommend someone."

He reached for her hands, sagged against the back of the sofa, and said, "Okay." He turned off the TV and began telling her all of what happened while he was deployed.

Chapter 10

Do not answer a fool according to his folly,
or you yourself will be just like him.
Proverbs 26:4 (NIV)

Angus had almost finished his shift when he and Sherman rounded the corner near the new pharmacy built a few months ago close to the town square. It was another one of those impersonal chain pharmacies advertising household items and quick service. Jean came over the radio.

"Angus, we got a code 33, noise nuisance at the Green Acres trailer park. Looks like Lucas is at it again. Lot 27."

Sherman drove across town, turned right at the light near the interstate, and pulled into the park, taking care to not drive over the glass beer bottles at the two stop signs within the park. It was a warm day, toddlers and their older siblings wandered the park in worn-out dirty clothes. Some kids waved at them as they drove slowly by, and one or two flipped them off.

"Green Acres? Should have named the place Wasteland Acres. It's spring and the only thing green are the weeds. Look at that lot. The yard's a jungle, it looks like its never been mowed. The weeds are as tall as the trailer," Sherman said shaking her head.

"Geez, it's sad people live like this. I feel for the kids," Angus said as they drove past "lawns" littered with trash, pop and beer cans everywhere. Dirty diapers and Walmart bags littered the area. One bag danced across the street and tried to attach to the squad car's wipers.

She pulled the car into number 27. They looked at the trailer, beer cans, tools and vehicle parts cluttered the sidewalk and yard. "Yup, this is it." Music emanated loudly from the trailer. *Highway to Hell* by AC/DC was blaring, causing the car's windows to shake.

"Highway to hell, looks like they already arrived," she said.

They got out of the squad car and walked to the trailer.

Angus knocked loudly on the door. Lucas peered from behind a hole in the cardboard covered window. His blue eyes narrowed when he saw it was the police.

"What do you want?"

"Open the door please," Sherman said.

Lucas opened the door, and the music became deafeningly louder. He had one of the current men's taper and fade hairstyles, shaved on the sides looking almost Hitler-esque. He was wearing jeans and a dingy wife-beater T-shirt with a cigarette dangling out of his mouth and a whiskey bottle in his hands.

"Lucas, turn the music down. There has been a complaint. Please lower the volume. We don't want to come here again," Angus said as loud as he could without yelling.

"Yah, yah," he said, "Must be old lady Jeffers. She is always calling on me." Sticking his head out the door he yelled, "Hey, old lady, you got a problem with me?" staring her down as she peaked through the sheer curtains yellowed with age and nicotine. She took a long drag of her cigarette, gave him the bird and turned away.

Sherman stepped aside on the rickety wooden deck, providing Angus the opportunity to glance inside. He grimaced when he saw Macey on the worn-out sofa. She tried to scamper away, but he definitely saw her. *What the*—? *What is she doing with this loser?* He would have to talk with Clara about Macey dating this jerk.

Lucas shut the door and turned the music down. Angus heard him scream something at Macey as they walked to the squad car and headed for the station.

***

Angus met Belissa at the bowling alley for their second date that week. He saw her pull in and once she parked, he walked over and opened her car door.

"Hey sugar," she said and gave him a peck on the cheek.

He was surprised at her greeting, especially after their argument over local politics the night before. "Let's get inside. It's Saturday and the place is bound to be packed."

After years of zoning issues, the bowling alley was added to the bar, The Prickly Pear. Built in the 1940s, it was one of a few genuine honky-tonks still in continuous operation.

Walking in he noticed a bright poster on the door announcing that tonight was karaoke night. *Hmm, I may slip in there later on. There's always someone who thinks they can sing.* "You want to sing some karaoke tonight after we bowl?"

"Lordy no. I have many talents but, singing isn't one of them." She pulled him near and gave him a prolonged kiss and then smiled up at him.

Inside, the alley was a din of noise. Arcade games whistled and dinged. Bowling pins reset and the smell of shoe spray disinfectant lingered in the air. Angus paid for their lane and grabbed their shoes.

"We're over there, lane eight." They sat down and changed into their bowling shoes.

"Eww, I hate these shoes. They're so germy." She wrinkled her nose in disgust.

"They spray them. I think you're safe from athlete's foot," and rolled his eyes at her.

Angus sat on a long plastic bench tying his laces, then stood to stretch. Clapping his hands together he declared, "All right, let's get started," and walked over and ran his hand over the cool air of the ball return.

"I don't want to play. I want to go to my place. Don't you?" she said flirting, and reached to run her fingers through his hair.

He removed her hands from his hair. "I've been looking forward to this. I haven't been bowling since I was in high school. Let's get a couple of games in. Then we can go. Okay?"

"Sure honey." She leaned in to get her ball from the machine.

"You're up."

"Why Angus I think I've forgotten how to bowl. Be a gentleman and come show me how."

He stood behind her, and she leaned her body into his. He'd never dated a woman so brazen. He knew many guys found it appealing but it was beginning to wear on him. He cleared his throat and backed away. He helped extend her arm and swing it back when she screamed.

Her cries filled the alley. "Look, look what you did. My nail broke off in the bowling ball's hole." She scowled at him and held her bleeding hand tightly. "I'm probably going to lose that nail. How's that going to look?"

"It was an accident."

"Now I've got to go to the car and get my purse to get a band aid and repair it." She shoved him out of her way and stomped to her car.

He shrugged his shoulders, "May as well get something to eat. Looks like this is going to be another disaster date," he said as he watched her storm off. Instead of ordering from the table intercom, he went to the bar to place the order and get them drinks.

It took a moment for his eyes to adjust to the darkened room. The smell of stale beer hit him as he stepped up to the counter. Music blared and he tapped his foot to the beat while watching a couple finish their slow dance. As they danced, the gentle swish of saw dust fibers filtered through the light of the neon signs. He took a bite of the stale pretzels offered as free appetizers and knocked them over when saw Clara, Bryan, and Macey at a table near the dance floor. His mind raced back to all the double dates they had and the fun they had together.

He scooped up the pretzels and put them back in the tiny faux wooden bowl.

A lanky man dressed in jeans, cowboy boots, and a loud paisley western shirt approached the dance floor, microphone in hand. "Howdy y'all, thanks for coming. My name is Bill and I'll be the KJ, Karaoke Jockey tonight. Karaoke will begin at 7:30. If you haven't already given your song and name to the bartender please do so now."

Angus looked around his sister had spotted him. *Guess I'd better say hello.* He walked over and sat next to Bryan. "Hey, y'all. I can't stay. Belissa is outside getting her purse to fix the nail she just broke bowling."

Macey took a sip of her soda and said nothing. Her heart fluttered, she looked away trying not to notice how good Angus looked in his jeans and tight T-shirt.

Bill announced, "Our first singer tonight is Macey. Please come up to the microphone."

This is going to be good. She's always had a great voice. I hope Belissa takes her time. Angus moved his chair in closer to the table and rested his chin in his hand. Macey whispered something in the man's ear. She stepped forward and sang Patsy Cline's song about lost love, "*She's Got You.*"

He grew uncomfortable, alternating between looking at her and peeling the label off his water bottle. *Could it be she cares? Nah, there's no way she'd ever forgive me. She's moved on. Guess I have to too. But dang she looks great. Get a grip man, it'll never happen.* His chest ached, the pain in her voice was evident for all to hear.

Clara and Bryan looked like they were at a tennis match each turning their heads from Macey to Angus and then back again.

Her voice caught and cracked at the last words of the song. Macey's eyes drilled into him, she hung her head and wiped away a reluctant tear.

Is that a tear? He sat there too stunned to move.

Clara grabbed a napkin, glared at her brother, and then jumped up to take Macey to the ladies room.

"Well, that went well," Bryan said, raising his eyebrows over his longneck beer. "Hate to tell you this, but your date has been watching the whole time."

Belissa emerged from the shadows and she was not pleased. A vein in her neck pulsated and she grimaced. Macey came walking back to the table just as Belissa sat on Angus' lap and nuzzled his neck.

"Sorry, it took a little longer than I thought. I had to fix my hair. Oh, Angus you smell divine. Let's finish our game." She gave him a hug, took his hand, and dragged him to the alley. But not before she looked back at Macey and flashed a devious look of triumph at her.

Angus' thoughts varied between Macey and their past. He regretted abandoning her when she was pregnant, and wondered what could have been if he weren't such an idiot years ago. His heart felt heavy, and he rubbed his temples. He felt a headache coming on.

"Angus, honey, your turn." She swatted his butt, "Those jeans look so good on you."

He raised the ball and got a strike. Belissa threw her arms around his neck and congratulated him with a kiss.

When he didn't respond the way she anticipated, she said, "What's wrong? You're thinking about her, aren't you?"

He tried to deny it. "No, I've got work on my mind."

Her eyes narrowed, and she picked up the ball. His body language spoke volumes, his eyes kept darting back to the bar. Frustrated, she yanked the ball from the ball return. Stepping to the red line, she dropped the heavy ball hard onto the wooden floor and watched it wiggle its way to the nearest gutter.

Before she could protest, he said, "Damn, I forgot our food. I told them I'd pick it up. Probably all cold by now. I'm going to get you another soda and place an order for fresh nachos."

He walked quickly to the bar. It took a moment for his eyes to adjust to the dark interior. Neon beer logos in blues and yellows flashed to the beat of the music. An annoyed bartender was at the other end of the long-horn skull and horns decorated bar. *Must be the horrible singers. Don't think I could listen to that all night.* A row of glistening liquor bottles behind the bar reflected the lights creating a prism of blues, greens, and reds.

"Wow, this one's got talent," Angus said sarcastically as a handsome man with a voice akin to nails on a chalkboard sang into the microphone. The crowd squirmed, some politely turning their heads away to escape the racket. He finally finished to meager applause.

"I hate karaoke night, it's the worst. What'll it be?"

"I need a water and an order of nachos."

"Sure thing."

"I'll wait here. Thanks," he said, and gave him the money for the drink and food.

Macey came around the corner and bumped into Angus. He turned. "Excuse me?" Seeing it was Macey he changed his demeanor. Her face was puffy and her eyes were red.

"Oh, sorry. I, I didn't see you there." She reached for a napkin. "Here let me help you with that." Big strong hands wrapped around hers, she trembled and looked up. "Sorry, Angus. I, I didn't realize it was you I bumped into."

Forgetting where he was, he looked down at her, and kept her hands in his. A jolt of electricity ran through his heart. *Is that a tear? Ah, man I made her cry...again.*

"Hey, I um, I'm really," he stammered.

"You're really what?" Belissa said. She stepped between them, arms crossed, "What was that you were going to say?"

Macey jerked her hands away. The electric current that held them together died, and any hope of reconciliation, like a broken and damaged fuse box, shocked Angus' mind and slowly burned away.

Macey made strong eye contact with him and said, "Yes, Angus what were you going to say?"

Great, I've ticked them both off. Way to go. "Never mind." He left the food at the bar. "Come on Belissa, let's leave this place."

Belissa attempted to protest but he shut her down.

Changing shoes, he said, "Get your things. I'm done." Unsure if he meant done with Belissa or done with his feelings for Macey.

"I can't believe you were talking to her and holding her hands," she said, emphasizing the word *and*. "You got a lot of nerve. That was so humiliating!" She covered her face and sobbed into her hands.

"It was nothing. You're overreacting." His facial muscles tightened.

"You're lying, I can tell." She stomped to her feet like a child.

"Let's just go. You're making a scene, an unnecessary scene."

"Oh really? Maybe I should announce to everyone what you just did? I bet every woman in this place would agree with me."

"Fine. I'm leaving. Stay or go. I don't care."

Realizing she had gone too far, she hurried after him. "Angus don't be angry with me. It's just, it's just that I can't help myself when I see her with you."

"Whatever," he said, and kept walking.

"I'll call you tomorrow, honey," she said as he got in the Bronco.

The cop in him prevented him from peeling out as he left the parking lot.

Chapter 11

The king said to Daniel, "Surely your God
is the God of gods and the Lord of kings and
a revealer of mysteries, for you were able to
reveal this mystery." Daniel 2:47 (NIV)

Angus finished eating his specialty burger loaded with bacon, avocado, and a fried egg on top at the only quasi-gourmet-gastro pub in town, The Side. It was the best burger joint in three counties. The proprietors had stenciled the large windows with beer mugs and burgers on the outside. Immense wooden tables allowed for large groups. Corrugated metal siding adorned the walls halfway up with rustic wooden beams interspersed with a cobblestone border.

Looking up, he admired the original tin ceiling that gave the place a comfy, homey feel. The food was delicious, well worth the $15 for a burger and fries.

Angus winked and flirted with the cute wait staff at the register. He so enjoyed a good flirt, and the opportunity to flash his smile. While paying the tab he saw Macey come through the big wood and iron bar door and get a table.

She wore her work scrubs, purple Crocs, and her long black hair fell like loose ribbons on her shoulders. *She always looks cute doesn't matter what she wears.* Her grandfather, Pops, headed towards the men's room. He wore a faded blue check shirt, jeans, cowboy boots and a hat, his long gray braid reaching to the middle of his back.

"Hello, Macey," he said smiling. "Pops, good to see you."

"Hi, Angus."

"Excuse me, Macey, but I need to use the facilities," Pops said as he ignored Angus on his way to the men's room at the back.

"Pops looks good. What's he doing?"

"He quit drinking and he's been on the wagon for about two months now. He's doing really good. Been going to church with me too. He just came from an AA meeting at the library, so I thought I would treat him to a burger to mark his second month of being sober."

"You always were too good to him. He doesn't deserve you," he said leaning against the checkout counter, smiling at the waitress and handing her his debit card.

"Everyone deserves kindness and forgiveness, Angus," Macey said.

"Well, I gotta go. See you." He didn't want to get into a conversation about forgiveness while still dealing with her abortion.

"Bye, Angus," Macey said with a tone of sadness.

It was lunch time, and the place was busy. Through the window Angus watched as Macey hurried over and grabbed the only free place, even though it had not been cleaned. The table was situated at a sizable window. He stared as streams of sunlight reflected the blue shine in her hair. He rushed back in and up to Macey.

Neither saw Belissa watching from across the street at The Kitchen Sink, a red brick building that had a brown and white striped awning, and served coffee, smoothies, and homemade, fresh-baked pastries. The coffee shop had a distinct hipster vibe, cactus greenery on the tables, and colorful chalkboard written menu items that meticulously described the organic smoothies and sandwiches. Near her, a green antique cupboard stood in the corner, its shelves filled with trade coffee blends, teas, and scones.

Belissa had stopped there to get a tall, iced mocha latte to satisfy her caffeine addiction. She watched Angus and Macey through the large plate-glass window. Observing Angus smiling, she assumed at Macey, but he was smiling about Pops being on the wagon. He grinned and winked at the buxom waitress who checked him out with her eyes while ringing up his meal at the register. *Oh, I am so going to talk to Angus about this, and when he's not looking, I'm going to check his phone log.* She turned to eat her croissant and saw a blur.

Are my eyes deceiving me? Angus walked back into the restaurant and over to Macey's table! "Oh no he didn't. Don't you dare do it, don't do it." She angrily tapped her long talon like nails on the windowsill. "Oh, he is so going to pay for this."

She pressed into the window at the bakery as if this could help her hear their conversation across the street better. Her arms glued to the window as angry breath caused frost to form on the cool glass.

Angus came back in and over to her table. *It's long over, why is my heart racing?"*

Macey tilted her head inquisitively and asked, "You're back?"

He took off his hat and placed his hands on the table, "Uh, yah, I wanted to give you a heads up about Lucas. He's bad news, Macey. You shouldn't be with him. He's a repeat offender. There's a long rap sheet on him for crimes like stealing manhole covers and empty beer kegs for scrap money and for shoplifting. He's suspected in several domestic abuse cases. His girlfriend's refuse to report him, too afraid I guess, and there are never any witnesses. Nothing good can come from you being with him."

"Well, ain't that rich?" Macey said as she motioned her head towards the window. "Nothing good can come of this conversation. There's Belissa, staring at us from across the street," Macey said with a touch of sarcasm mixed with a Southern drawl. "She's cray cray Angus. You better be careful with her."

He saw Pops coming back, and not wanting to continue this conversation in public with him around, he tipped his hat and left quickly.

Belissa stood by the window, swallowing hard to control the internal volcano about to erupt. Concentrating, she choked back the acidy lava words. Maintaining her composure, she said aloud, "Oh, he is *really* going to pay for this." She gulped her latte and slammed it onto the counter by the window causing the coffee to spurt out the top and onto the floor as she left the bakery.

***

Anne finished clearing the chef salad she and Will had for lunch from the table. She looked at his plate and again at Will noting he didn't eat most of the "rabbit food" as he called it.

She placed the dishes in the farmers sink and went back to the table and sat next to him. "I've been thinking about Belissa these past few days."

"Um hmm, like what?" He straightened his paper not paying much attention.

"She was always a happy child until her father left them for another woman."

"That was pretty bad."

"I'm sure it affected her emotionally."

From behind the paper he said, "Isn't that around the time she got involved in the occult stuff?"

"Yes, Clara said she'd read Tarot cards and would make up imaginary spells to cast on the girls who teased her about her weight."

"Um hmm."

"Belissa has changed so much and not for the better. She's so angry. I can see it in her eyes. I'm really concerned about her and Angus. Can I tell you about a dream I had a few nights ago?"

"Sure, I'm all ears," he said putting his paper down. Though unusual for others, Will knew God spoke to Anne through dreams when she struggled with an issue.

"Well, I went down to the basement, and with each step I took, the stairs and the walls turned to a gray, slippery stone. The walls had condensation on them, but instead of them being cool, they were blistering hot. The air had an awful dead smell and it made breathing difficult. The odor was so overwhelming, I almost started gagging. I took each step cautiously, fearing I would fall into an abyss near the bottom of the steps. I remember thinking I didn't want to be caught looking in." She took a sip of Will's drink and continued.

I reached the bottom of the steps and turned to the left, and there on the walls were all sorts of moving shadows. One of the shadows—it must have been a demon—came out from the wall. It slithered and then morphed into a grotesque, terrifying creature with scales and feathers. The hideous beast had broken limbs bent at odd angles, drooling blood, and as it crawled, it made fiendish garbled and growling noises. I don't know how to describe what I saw. It was a man and woman monstrosity, with tatts of goats, pentagrams, and upside-down crosses on its arms.

I peered in and Angus was laying on a giant slab of a black granite table! He smiled at the thing, a horrid-looking gargoyle-type thing. This, this thing," she stammered, "sat on top of Angus, almost stifling his breathing. But here's what's weird, it smiled at him and leaned over his face, turning its head to the left then right, smirking and sneering, showing its fangs, and it had row after row of sharp teeth like a shark. It lunged for Angus' jugular and I said, 'Stop. Angus, wake up!' He looked at me and said, 'But, Mom, it's my friend.' Then I woke up. What on earth could this dream mean?"

"I think I know, Anne. You were right in being concerned about Angus seeing Belissa. She is not the same girl we knew years ago. When she was here, I saw her pull her shirt sleeve up, and I noticed she had tattoos of goats, pentagrams, and upside-down crosses on her arm. This can't be good. I believe we need to pray for our son *and* for Belissa."

Will and Anne bowed their heads right there at the table and prayed earnestly for the two.

***

Angus stared at his phone. "Geez," he muttered. "Stop calling Belissa," he said silencing his cell.

He spent the last day or so analyzing their relationship. He needed another guy's opinion and decided he would ask Mark the next time he saw him.

While working a game at the high school, Angus spotted Mark at the other end of the gym, standing at the entrance and hurried over to him. "Hey, Mark, thanks for working the playoff game on such short notice. Listen, I want to run something past you and get your thoughts."

"Sure, what's going on?" Mark asked as he sipped his soda.

He played back the dates, movies, dinner, the car show, and lunches. "I wish I would have listened to my sister. If it were near the holidays it'd be much easier to break up."

"The holidays, what do you mean?"

"In previous relationships I always broke up some-time after Halloween but before Thanksgiving, prefer-ably on a Friday night. Fridays are the best because it gives them the weekend to collect themselves before work on Monday. I never date anyone seriously from November through February. I can save money, and not end up giving a gift that sends the wrong message."

"Like what?"

"Well, at Thanksgiving the girls are always trying to get you to meet their family. Too much commitment there, then Christmas…what do you give? Perfume and slinky lingerie is too intimate, jewelry is definitely out. Bracelet, earrings, doesn't matter, they start talking and the next thing you know they're seeing wedding bells. New Years, means new resolutions to work on the 'relationship'," he said as he did air quotes. Then the ultimate, Valentine's Day." He shook himself as the thought of the holidays gave him the shivers and continued. "Nope, no holidays for me, and since it's late summer no need to worry about those rules with Belissa." He dug his thumbs into his leather duty belt.

"Mark, she is nuts. I do whatever I can to keep her happy and anything to prevent an explosion. Heck, I even went clothes shopping with her *and* held her purse! It seems every date we go on—we've been dating for almost two months—starts out good and ends up with her ticked off and angry at me for the littlest things. If she isn't complaining, she's fiddling with her hair. I can't touch it without getting my hand swatted."

"What does she get upset about?"

"It's stuff like playing the wrong song or not remem-bering we passed the one-month anniversary or me not commenting on her new top. It's exhausting, man. Every date is always a guessing game, a game I can never win."

"Wow, she's got you," Mark said.

The thought hit him like a slap to the face. "She's trying to control me. How could I have been so dumb? I'm an emotional hostage constantly being interrogated, never knowing if I'll be hit with a verbal barrage of unrealistic and impossible demands."

He adjusted his heavy belt and sighed. "Mark, this clearly is not working." He tried to imagine ways to break it off, maybe he'd ghost her, but with them both living in the same small town, that wasn't possible. The thought of cheating crossed his mind but it wasn't in his DNA, and there was always the slow fade. Angus stood arms crossed, contemplating, deep in the weeds of his relationship, when he came to the uncomfortable conclusion he would have to man up and do it in person.

***

In an attempt to avoid Belissa, Angus worked as many extra jobs as he could. He had picked up a job at the high school basketball playoff game against the town's arch rivals a week later.

While at the concession stand chatting with an old friend, he saw Belissa enter the building wearing her usual high-heeled black buckled boots, and leggings. A glittery skull-embossed top hugged her curves. Her teased hair was piled high in a messy bun; she looked good, but he knew she was not worth the drama. He pivoted, trying to hide behind his friend to avoid her, she had spotted him.

Almost running, he headed back to the gymnasium. He walked fast taking big strides. The faster he walked, the faster she rushed toward him, waving her arms in the air to get his attention, practically running to him calling out his name.

"Angus, hey, Angus, honey," she yelled, somehow catching up to him.

"Why, Angus, if I didn't know any better, I'd say you are ignoring me," she said breathlessly.

"Hello, Belissa, was that you hollering? Sorry, I didn't notice."

She did not try to hide her anger, and clenching her fists and jaw said, "I could see you talking to Macey the other day at The Side. Don't lie to me. What were you talking about? Are you seeing her too? You'd better not be double dipping, Angus. I will make you pay for two-timing me." She grabbed his arm and dug her long pointy claw-like nails into him. She concentrated, choking back the vulgar words trying to come out of her mouth and spew at Angus. She had rehearsed this moment and was eager to put him in his place in front of everyone in the gym. Her latte sloshed as she punctuated her words, pointing her finger at his chest. Her coffee spurted out and onto his uniform.

"Geez, be careful," he said and then quietly let out an expletive under his breath. "Belissa, do we have to have this conversation now? Here? Can't it wait until after the game?" He wanted to let her down gently, but that wasn't happening.

"Angus, I can see you're working, but this can't wait. I demand you tell me what you were talking about with Macey. She can't have you. You belong to me." She stood in defiance with her hands on her hips as bitter tears trickled down, smudging her makeup.

When she said belong, he almost lost his composure Fuming he managed to maintain it. He had no choice, he was on the job. No longer trying to hide his frustration, he gritted his teeth and muttered, "She's right, you are cray cray."

"Excuse me? What did Macey say about me? You let her talk that way? You didn't stop her?"

"Listen, Belissa, I really don't want to do this here, but you are pushing the issue, so I may as well tell you. It's over."

He smugly believed she would eventually move on. All his previous girlfriends did, each one handling the breakups poorly. Most called for a month or two, leaving messages asking, "What did they do wrong?" and imploring him to give it another chance. The neediness got on his nerves, so he'd ignore their pleas until eventually the calls would stop. Trying to catch him at work, the brokenhearted ex-girlfriends would call the station. Some even called his buds hoping to speak to him when they were out at a game or whatever. He let out a huff and with conceit thought, *Yup, I am hard to get over, but hey I need to spread the love and move on. I'm a good catch; just not ready for marriage yet.* He didn't want to give her an opportunity to discuss this further. She needed to digest the news alone, without him around.

He pretended he saw a scuffle and left her in the hallway crying.

"Angus Connors, how dare you! You will regret this," she yelled.

***

Belissa stormed out of the building in a rage, almost knocking over a booster club parent as she swung the glass door open. She got to her car and sped out of the parking lot, nearly running over a pedestrian on the way to her place above Joey's.

Every Friday night was karaoke night at Joey's and there were no empty tables. Belissa walked in and ordered a hard cider, took a long, deep drink, and noticed Lucas sitting alone at the bar. A bottle blonde, in a tight knit top gripped the microphone stand for balance as she slurred a love song to her boyfriend near the bar. Belissa knew Lucas was a loser. She had caught him loading Joey's empty kegs into a pickup truck. Thankfully, he never figured out she called the police. It didn't matter, misery loved company, and she hated being alone. Anyone would do, even Lucas.

"Hey, Lucas, whatcha doin?" she said as she slid next to him on the vacant barstool.

He eyed her and then said, "I can't believe she did it."

"Who did what?"

"Macey, we've been dating off and on for about three months now. This afternoon when I went by her lousy grooming place, she told me she didn't want to date me anymore. Said it would never work out because she started going back to church and got the stupid idea

113

our relationship was wrong. She didn't even cry. Then get this, she said all high and mighty that bad company corrupts good morals. I hate to admit it, but I was wasting my time on her."

"Well, I can relate. Angus dumped me in front of everyone at the basketball game of all places. He couldn't be decent about it and do it privately. No, not him." Her eyes squinted as she continued to exaggerate their breakup. "He was in such a rage he just about slapped me. He stormed off when he saw someone coming. I don't know how I'll do it, but I'm going to get my revenge. Nobody dumps me."

"Here's to revenge," Lucas said taking a swig from the bottle.

They spent the remainder of the night huddled next to each other, dreaming and plotting of ways to extract revenge on Angus and Macey. Bottles were raised as they gleefully toasted the others ruthlessness. Before the bar closed, they had become the closest of friends.

Chapter 12

Whoever slanders their neighbor in secret,
I will put to silence;
whoever has haughty eyes and a proud heart,
I will not tolerate. Psalm 101:5 (NIV)

Angus answered his phone. "Hello."

"How are you doing, sweetie?"

"Good, Mom. I'm a little busy at the moment. What's up?" he said as he motioned to Jean to act like there was a call coming in, which to his dismay she ignored.

"I know what you can get me for Mother's Day."

"What?"

"You can go with us to church," she said with a lilt in her voice. She held her breath hoping for the remote possibility he would agree.

"Um, uh, I, yah sure," he said as he looked over a police file.

"Oh, son, that would be great, and afterward we can all go out to eat. Your dad has made lunch reservations somewhere."

"Okay, see you soon," and ended the call. *Great, just great. Why, oh why, did I agree to that? I keep my word, so there's no way to get out of it.* He smirked when he realized he wouldn't have to go through the rigmarole and buy his mom a gift.

***

Angus rose early Mother's Day morning, showered, then pressed and put on his long-sleeve paisley blue with coordinating cuffs designer shirt—his favorite. He brushed his teeth, and admired his new haircut that tamed his thick hair. Looking in the mirror, he paused and said aloud, "Damn, I'm hotter than fresh buttered biscuits."

He grabbed a quick slice of toast, slathered it with butter and his mom's homemade strawberry jam, and hovered over the sink—bachelor style as he ate. He inhaled deeply of the coffee's strong aroma, yawned and hoped the caffeine could keep him awake. He squeezed his eyes shut and grimaced, mentally preparing for what he felt would be a boring and dragged out church service. Stuffing his car keys in his pocket, he took a dirty travel mug from the cluttered sink rinsed it and poured the brew, no sugar, only creamer, and headed out the door.

It was a beautiful Mother's Day—an eye-squinting sunny and warm morning. Already he regretted the promise he made to his mom. He would rather watch a game, any game, instead of going to church, but he kept his word and left for the service.

He drove through town in no hurry, not wanting to be too early, and definitely not wanting to have to deal with the all the comments from his parents' friends like, "Angus, I haven't seen you in a month of Sundays. Ain't you a sight for sore eyes, and wherever have you been?" He drove through the quiet streets, and kept an eye open for anything unusual or out of place. He couldn't escape being a cop.

He rounded the last corner before the church and recognized Lucas outside the town drugstore in an argument with a woman. She was standing, waving her arms in the air, poking her finger at his chest. Lucas leaned into the woman, glared at her, and raised his voice, letting out a string of expletives. As Angus drove past them, Lucas retreated to his rusty pickup truck.

The woman scowled, took a long drag from her cigarette, turned sharply, and jerked the pharmacy door open without saying another word.

"Hmm, I wonder what that's all about." Angus made a mental note to ask nosey Jean to see what he could find out. But for now, he had to get to church.

He pulled into the church's parking lot, hurried to find a spot. With it being Mother's Day, there weren't many spaces left. "Humph, holiday Christians," he muttered.

Funny how he never thought of including himself in the same group, and there was no reason why he would—he never went to church no matter the holiday. Thankfully he found a slot next to his parents' car. As he rushed to greet them, he almost banged their car door when he opened his. Angus squinted at the sun's brightness and pulled on his shades. He noticed his parents near the entry and hurried over to hug them. They were about to enter the church, and he scurried to hold the door, giving each a quick hug as they stepped into the foyer.

An old dented drinking fountain was next to the women's restroom door. Sparse plastic greenery near the men's room was in direct contrast with the fresh flowers decorating the foyer. Children ran about excited, dodging each other as parents tried to corral them for pictures.

"Oh, Lordy, there she is, Bertha better than you," his dad said, as Mrs. Grobbles and her ilk passed by.

"Shh, Will, she'll hear you," his mom said.

His dad paused, took a deep breath, looked up the ceiling and said, "Lord, could you please take her home today?"

"Will!" his mother said poking him in the ribs.

"Anne, you and I both know what she is like. She is so mean-spirited she and her friends have driven two pastors away. Her native tongue is complaint, and she speaks fluent gossip. People like her are a bad witness."

"Ain't that the truth," Angus agreed. "Because she's wealthy she bosses people around."

"Don't I know it, son. Every time she gives a big donation she tries to put stipulations on the money."

"You two keep your voices down." Anne put her finger to her lips making a shh sound. "Will don't try to hide your unforgivenss with humor."

"Dad, I remember how she made our lives miserable when Uncle Robert left with the church secretary. Didn't you two have a huge argument about it?"

"Yes, we did, when I stood up to her and told her we had nothing to do with it, she tried to get me removed from the Elder board."

"It's probably guilt by association in her mind," Angus added staring in her direction. "People like her are one of the reasons why I don't go to church anymore."

"Will, stop it. I think pastor can handle her, and besides the Lord can spank that puppy better than you can. You need to let it go, the things she did to us are in the past. Remember to forgive. 'Sides you know as well as I that hurt people, hurt people," Anne said shaking her head, digging through her purse. "Oh where is my lipstick?" She paused long enough to apply it and then took Will's arm and started walking to the sanctuary, but changed her mind.

"You two go ahead, I need to use the ladies room."

Angus and his father entered the long hallway leading to the sanctuary. Angus held his breath and froze when he noticed both Macey and Belissa coming through the glass doors at the same time. "Oh boy." He ducked and tried to disappear behind a large wooden column. *This is going to be interesting.*

Listening from behind the column, Angus could hear Mrs. Grobbles and her followers circle in, heads bowed discussing the audacity of Belissa to show up at church.

He heard someone say, "Can you believe she has the nerve to come here? Why, she's into witchcraft! It will disrupt the flow of the service." Another agreed and said, "It will stifle the Holy Spirit." Someone commented, "Look, there's Macey! And she brought her drunk grandfather. I mean really? And her dress...why it's as ugly as homemade sin."

Mrs. Grobbles said, "Honestly, what are they doing here? It's Mother's Day, all these visitors and she shows up with the town drunk! It wouldn't surprise me if he passed out at the altar. And we *all* know what she did years ago." She creased her brows and wrinkled her nose in disgust as the entire group shot looks of revulsion at Macey.

Angus wanted to say something and tried to control himself.

He couldn't just think about it. Every inch of him wanted to set the scheming, malicious witch straight. He felt his jugular vein throb and his face flushed with anger and he walked over to her. "I gotta say, Mrs. Grobbles, you don't discriminate. You gossip about everybody. I ain't no churchgoer, but everyone knows gossiping is flat out wrong. Remember what the Bible says, the tongue is a restless evil full of deadly poison, and I might add yours is overflowing!"

It got the reaction he had hoped for. She marched off in a huff, with her groupies following close behind saying she wasn't going to stand for this.

"Hey, then sit," Angus said loud enough for Mrs. Grobbles and everyone surrounding her to hear. He turned to see his mom emerging from the restroom.

"Wow, Mom, you sure took a long time."

"I was giving Mrs. Green my nanner pudding recipe. We'd better hustle in. What did I hear you say to Mrs. Grobbels?"

"Nothing I was setting her straight."

"You seem proud of yourself."

He blushed and knew he'd gone too far. "Mom, I just can't abide that woman."

"You need to remember that she's been through a lot and remember that as you have been forgiven so you should forgive. Unforgiveness poisons the soul." She turned to give him a peck on the cheek then held her elbow out to be escorted to their seat.

Angus greeted the ushers and studied the crowd, trying to find his dad. With the church being so full, he wasn't in his usual seat, three rows from the front. He craned his neck and found him in the pew right in front of Mrs. Grobbles. He caught a glare from her as they passed her pew.

Angus sat down, feeling the heat from Mrs. Grobble's angry stare burning into his back.

A group of energetic people came to the platform, taking various positions. Angus watched with keen interest. *Well, this certainly isn't how I remembered church. It used to be only a pianist and someone on guitar when I was a kid.*

There were at least five singers—three women and two men—and a drummer behind a noise reduction plastic soundproof booth. At the rear of the stage area stood two beefy bass players, and a well-dressed man his parents' age on the keyboard.

The lights were dimmed, the cross illuminated on the platform. The music started and everyone stood, some raised their hands, while others clapped. Angus rose thinking this is almost like a concert. The music was upbeat, and the musicians were talented. No old ladies warbling on a piano here, Angus noted as little kids clapped and danced about in the aisles. Even the elderly stood, and if possible, raised their hands, with looks of gratitude on their weathered faces. Congregants old and young, expensively dressed, in cowboy boots, or flip-flops, it didn't matter—each was absorbed in worship.

Angus stood, clapped his hands, trying to sing along to songs he wasn't familiar with. He struggled through most of them. His heart froze when he recognized Macey two rows in front with Pops. Both were engrossed in the music, hands lifted, faces looking upward, lost in song.

He turned to his right and noticed Belissa and her mom across the aisle. *Mrs. Baker, sure looks elated. Hmm must be glad Belissa is in church.* He turned toward Belissa and saw an entirely different picture. She stood with arms crossed, agitatedly rapping her fingers on the pew in frustration as if doing so would speed along the service. She'd stand then sit and then sit and stand again looking around bored.

It had been about a few months since their breakup. Belissa called Angus numerous times, leaving messages telling him how much she loved and missed him. The next day he would find a barrage of voicemails saying she hated him, and how dare he treat her this way. Twice she called the station upset, requesting help, but Jean knew Belissa from her previous illicit affair with one of the station's former officers, so she curtly took the calls and promptly dispatched Sherman instead of Angus to Joey's.

After announcements, prayer, and the offering, Pastor Bill came to the podium in his usual Sunday morning attire crisp jeans and jacket and then began. "In keeping with Mother's Day, I'd like to begin with a quote from Erma Bombeck. 'When your mother asks,

"Do you want a piece of advice?" It is a mere formality. It doesn't matter if you answer yes or no. You're going to get it anyway.'" After a few laughs, he paused and asked the congregation to stand for the reading of God's word.

"Open your Bibles and turn with me to John 1:16, 'For of His fullness we have received grace upon grace.' Please be seated. You may be wondering what does John 1:16 have to do with moms? Moms have many special attributes God has given them. One of those attributes is grace. Moms, like God, have a great capacity for extending grace. Mothers give unmerited favor when we don't deserve it much like God does. But grace has a deeper meaning. The Greek word for grace is *chesed*. It means daily guidance, preservation, and enablement. Both God and Moms guide and instruct their children, enabling them to overcome difficult tasks and events in their lives. Moms and God both love to give good gifts. James 1:17 says 'Every good gift and every perfect gift is from above.' Be assured the manner in which God gives a gift is lavish, there's no reluctance with Him."

Pastor Bill walked over to his elderly mother, dressed in a pale lavender outfit that had a matching hat. He gently took her by the elbow to help her to her feet. "Stand up please, Momma." Beaming with pride Momma stood and waved. "My momma will tell you it was no easy task raising me. And I know personally a few of you have given your momma fits, yet moms continue loving."

Walking about the aisles, he held his Bible high, punctuating each sentence by thrusting it in the air. "God's love and your mother's love are unconditional. Your mother gave you life, she brought you into the world, and so it goes with God. He created you, for you are fearfully and wonderfully made. God knows the number of every hair on your head. While a mother's love is steadfast, enduring and kind, it could never compare to God's unchanging, unrelenting, reckless love for you. You see, he gave you the best gift ever, the gift of his son Jesus Christ. God died for you so you could become a member of the family of God."

Angus squirmed he felt uneasy as if Pastor was boring into his soul.

"Would you please consider all God has done for you and accept the gift of salvation? Be cleansed, set free from the bondages of sin. If you want to begin life anew and experience God's grace and marvelous gift, please raise your hand."

Angus noticed one or two hands go up, and a few were crying as the pianist played Amazing Grace.

Pastor then asked everyone to repeat after him. "Father God, for too long I have ignored you and tried to live my life by my own standards, I have made a mess of things. I know I am a sinner and I cannot save myself. Thank you for your marvelous gift of salvation. I thank you that Christ died for my sins when it should have been me on the cross. Thank you for taking away my sins. Thank you, Jesus, for coming to earth, I know you are the son of God who died and rose again from the dead. I ask you to come into my heart and be my Savior. Amen."

He paused and scanned the congregation. "Raising your hands was the first step, but now you need to confess your acceptance of Christ. I would love nothing better than to meet you. Won't you please come forward so my staff and I can give you further guidance?"

Angus sat wondering about his own life, internally reaching for a reason to respond to pastor's prayer for salvation. He rubbed his forehead, eyes closed, and recalled what happened to Kolby, his uncle's affair, and Macey's abortion.

The struggle was real. Eternal forces fought for and against him. His cell phone rang and he stirred from his thoughts. Embarrassed, he silenced his phone. Looking around, he hoped no one but him noticed. His mouth fell open when he spotted Lucas at the back, pacing. He seemed nervous but left before the end of the altar call. Angus stood as people came forward for prayer. He caught a glimpse of Macey kneeling at the altar, her hands outstretched toward heaven, praying. Fat tears rolled down her face as her lips moved silently.

Angus surmised she was asking God's forgiveness for the abortion; it did not occur to him he played a part in her decision. He glanced at Belissa who stood, then collected her purse and phone.

"Come on, Mom, let's go. I have dinner ready at my place," Belissa said as she all but pushed her mom out the aisle.

From the way she is fidgeting it looks like she wants to leave more than I do. I don't think that's a good sign for either of us.

His parents stayed back for a moment to chat with some friends, and Angus walked up to Macey and Pops. Before he could say a word, his mom said to Mrs. Green,

"I see someone I need to talk to." She walked over to Macey and sidled next to Angus and said, "Excuse me."

"Macey, would you and Pops like to join us for Mother's Day brunch? We are going to the Water's Edge Restaurant. We'd be delighted if you two could come."

"We would love to join you, uh, but I am not sure if Angus would be comfortable with that," she said.

"Oh, nonsense, you're coming."

"Angus, be a dear and give Macey a ride to the restaurant, please? Pops, you can ride along with Will and me. We would enjoy your company," she said as she looped her arm around Pops' elbow and guided him to their car.

***

"You know, Anne, you are shameless trying to get those two back together," Will said.

"I can't help myself. I can feel it in my bones. Those two are meant to be together, and someone has to push Angus into action. When it comes to all things love related, he can be so stubborn," she said as Will opened her car door.

People outside getting into their cars stopped, and those standing in the parking lot stared as an ambulance grew closer, its siren wailing as it pulled into the church parking lot.

The ambulance came to an abrupt stop at the entrance. An attendant threw open the doors, grabbed a gurney and pushed through the wondering crowd.

"She's in here," Pastor Bill yelled. "Hurry!"

"What happened?" Will asked.

"Tonya moaned and clutched her belly in the sanctuary. She doubled over and fell to the floor," someone said.

Anne hurried to where Tonya lay collapsed on the sanctuary floor holding her abundant belly, crying in pain. Kolby knelt next to Tonya grasping her hand, smiling tentatively as he brushed a stray hair from her sweaty and furrowed brow. Members of the congregation paced and prayed, asking God for divine healing and protection for the twins she was carrying.

The EMS worker took her vitals, blood pressure, and temperature, asking her how far along she was, and if she was having difficulty breathing, and where exactly was her pain.

They helped her up and loaded her on to the gurney. Kolby rushed down the hallway beside her, while Pastor Bill and Portia, his in-laws, collected their things and raced to their cars, waiting to follow the ambulance. The attendants loaded Tonya into the ambulance, slammed the doors shut as sirens blared, sped out of the parking lot, and headed to the hospital.

"Oh dear, oh dear," Anne said. "We had better forget about brunch and head to the hospital."

On the way over, Anne called Clara and Angus to let them know what had happened and to meet them at County Hospital.

***

Their hands brushed when Angus opened Macey's door. His body felt the electric shock of her touch. *She still does that to me.* The conversation on the way over was stilted, neither wanting to open up their hearts just yet. He was working up the courage to ask Macey out, trying to figure a good segue into asking when his cell phone rang.

"Hi, Mom, what's up?"

"Tonya has collapsed at the church. The ambulance is taking her to County. We'll meet you there. You'd better hurry. It doesn't look good."

"What, really? What happened?"

"She was standing next to Kolby and then she fell to the floor grabbing her belly. We'll know more at the hospital. Hurry."

"Okay, bye," he said.

Macey sensed the concern in his voice and asked, "What's going on?"

"Change of plans, Tonya collapsed at church, and the ambulance is taking her to County. We need to get there ASAP." Angus pulled the siren from the center console, placed it on the roof and sped to the hospital.

Angus glanced over and saw Macey's lips moving silently and her eyes closed. He hoped she could grab God's attention, and he threw in a few heartfelt prayers to God also.

Chapter 13

Children are a heritage from the LORD,
offspring a reward from him. Psalm 127:3 (NIV)

Bryan and Clara were already at the emergency room when Angus and Macey arrived, as were both Tonya's and Angus' parents.

The EMT team filled in the ER staff as the attending doctor and nurse took Tonya's vitals. They lifted her from the gurney onto the bed while Kolby and her parents looked on.

"What's happening?" Tonya moaned while her mother questioned the obstetrician on call.

"It might be several things. It may be as simple as overexertion or as serious as cord entanglement or the start of placental abruption. I won't know until I run some tests. Right now, her vitals are good." He lifted the sheet the EMTs had covered her with. "I'm not seeing signs of bleeding, but I still have to perform an exam. For now, I'll order an ultrasound and blood work. In the meantime, we will start a simple IV catheter in case we have to get meds to her quickly."

Doctor Chad, the obstetrician on call asked, "Can anyone tell me the name of her obstetrician? When was her last ultrasound?"

"I had one at 16 weeks, and it's Doctor Bergstrom." Tonya moaned.

"Okay, I need to call him. Please excuse me." He hurried off to the nurses' station to place the call.

"Portia and I, and the rest of us are going to the chapel to pray. Call me if there are any changes." Her father said, then hugged Kolby and left. Kolby stayed at her side, smiling feebly as he wiped her brow.

Pastor gathered everyone together in the waiting area and explained what the doctor said, before leading them to the chapel.

The quiet chapel was on the first floor near the main entrance to the hospital. To accommodate several Christian beliefs, there was an altar in the back with votive candles burning. Eight small pews with attached kneeling cushions were in the center, and several Bible versions were in each pew.

The group gathered together at the front, held hands, and entreated God, asking for his protection over Tonya and the twins, wisdom for the doctors and nurses, and for a good report on all tests. Pastor's voice cracked as he led a prayer, casting out fear, asking for healing and health. At the end everyone hugged and headed back to the ER.

Angus rushed in with Macey at his side. Before a nurse at the station could stop him and ask questions, he flashed his badge and strode to Kolby and gave him a brief hug. "Do you need anything? Can I get you a soda, maybe?"

"Nah, not right now. I know you aren't into prayer, but if you could, please pray. It would help a lot. I'd appreciate it."

"Of course, cheese head."

Kolby grinned, and Tonya gave a small chuckle and smiled up at them. Macey leaned in and gave her a quick hug and a tissue to wipe the tear trickling down her face.

***

Making their way to the chapel, Angus and Macey saw the others returning. They paused, and everyone exchanged hugs as the two continued on to the chapel.

Angus held the door for Macey, and they both entered quietly.

His heart beat wildly in his chest, he took her by the hand, pleased she didn't pull away. "Um, I don't know how to say this. Uh, I would understand if you are uncomfortable with me and the baby-danger situation."

They stood facing each other, both afraid of the possibilities. "Baby danger? What a weird way of putting a possible miscarriage. But really, I'm okay. She's my friend. I don't want anything bad to happen to her or the babies. I think you are concerned about me and the abortion more so than Tonya's babies. Is that what you are concerned about?"

He dropped his chin to his chest and said, "I don't want to cause you any more pain in that area."

She stepped closer. "It's okay, I went through a lot of heartache over the abortion. For the longest time I wasn't able to forgive myself. I don't deserve it, but He forgave me." She looked up and said, "Imagine, I took His treasured irreplaceable creation, his gift to me and killed my baby. When I couldn't forgive myself, He reached down and forgave me. He forgave me." She placed her hands over her heart. "Can you forgive me?"

He winced, her words hit him like a sucker punch, and his stomach knotted up. "I gotta be honest with you, I struggled a lot with what you did. It took me awhile, but I forgave you. I mean, I played a part in it also. I didn't have to ignore my parents and Clara. I was immature and made it all about me. Can you forgive me?"

"It took a while but I forgave you long ago. Forgiving myself was a much longer process. Really, it's okay, but thanks for caring. I appreciate it." Her heart fluttered as she reached for his hand. "If I didn't know any better, I'd say you still have feelings for me. Do you?"

After a long pause, he took a deep breath and whispered, "Yes, I still do. Always have."

"What about you and Belissa?"

"Ah, that's been over for a while."

Macey smiled and reached for his hands and led him to a pew. Apprehensive, he fidgeted and scrunched his eyes shut, concentrating he put his hands together, leaned forward and prayed. Remembering the last time Angus had talked to God was when he found out Macey was pregnant.

"God, this is Angus, but I guess you know that. It's been a long time." He continued and asked for God's mercy and for healthy babies. It was a short and sincere prayer. He smiled noticing an inner peace he hadn't had in quite a while certain everything would turn out for the good.

He cleared his throat and stood, signaling to Macey he had finished praying. Taking her hand, he gave it a quick squeeze, and they walked out of the chapel together, both beaming.

He stopped in the hallway. "Do you want to go out this Thursday? I'm off. I can pick you up on the Res, and we can go out of town to get a bite to eat. Somewhere we can talk with no one overhearing our conversation."

"Sure, Angus, I would love to, but I don't live on the Res anymore. I live across from the elementary school with Pops, the little red brick house opposite the bus loading area." Looking up at him her heart melted, and her face flushed at his gaze.

"Okay, great. How does six sound?"

"That sounds fantastic, Angus."

They walked in silence, hand in hand, each heart racing as they headed towards the waiting area. Anne spied the two as they approached the ER area.

"Will," Anne said as she grabbed his hand and pointed in their direction. They both grinned and tried not to appear obvious as they spied Angus and Macey holding hands.

With a clipboard in hand the doctor pulled back the curtain, and approached the bedside to discuss the test results with Kolby and Tonya.

"Let me begin by allaying your fears. Tonya is not about to miscarry nor is she beginning a placental abruption."

"Well, doc, what is it then?" Kolby asked.

"What's happening to me?"

"Your last ultrasound showed two heartbeats and because your doctor doesn't have the latest ultrasound equipment and because this can sometimes happen though rare—"

"What, what are you trying to say, doc?" Tonya asked.

"Um, well, there is an extra heartbeat the sonogram didn't detect." The doc let his last statement sink in.

Shocked, Kolby said, "Oh, boy, um, are you saying there's another baby?"

"Yes, she's having triplets!"

Kolby slapped his thigh, let out a whoop, and danced a little jig laughing.

Tonya, however, groaned. "I don't think my body can take another one in there. I get little sleep now, I can't get comfortable, and all I do is eat and go to the bathroom." She cried, "I can't see my toes or put shoes on now, and you're saying I am pregnant with triplets? I'll get bigger?"

"Tonya," he said and patted her arm, "you'll be fine. I will put you on bed rest, no lifting, and no house work for you."

A visible difference came over Kolby's appearance, his smile washed away when he realized he would have to pull double duty. Still, with the help of family and friends he knew they'd get through.

"Well, I am happy and envious of Dr. Bergstrom. Wish I could be there when he delivers them. Ah, well, I am off to call him and give him the news. He will be thrilled. It's rare when a doctor delivers triplets." He stood and gave Kolby his hand and left.

Kolby leaned over and gave Tonya a kiss and almost floating on air, he ran to the waiting room.

Unable to contain himself, as soon as the others saw him, he blurted out, "It's triplets!"

"Triplets?" Pastor and Portia said astonished.

Angus gave Kolby a slap on the back and said, "Impressive cheese head, mighty impressive."

Not waiting for the okay from either the doctor or the nurse, Tonya's parents, along with Clara and Macey, raced to her bedside.

Clara and Macey squealed, "Okay, let's discuss the shower."

"No, wait." Tonya straightened and tried to sit, grabbing the bed rails for support. "We need to talk about the logistics. We need three of *everything*! Let's be practical. We need to talk about helping Kolby with the cooking and cleaning. The good Lord knows he's a horrid cook and can't clean worth a lick. Leave the laundry to him, and all the clothes will be weird shades of greens and reds. He thinks you can throw everything into the washer all at once."

Anne pulled back the curtain. "Oh, it's getting crowded in here." She nudged Clara to scoot over. As Kolby, Angus, and pastor left the ER bay, they could hear each of the women talking and laughing with much joy and anticipation about the triplets.

Chapter 14

He who finds a wife finds what is good
and receives favor from the LORD.
Proverbs 18:22 (NIV)

While Angus loved the unusually warm weather—sticky, humid and overcast in the low-80s, typical for West Virginia—most folks hoped for a clear breezy day for their Labor Day holiday.

Angus had an ongoing conversation with himself about his relationship with Macey. He popped over to his folk's house to ask his dad a few questions. Though he hated to admit it, if anyone knew about having a good marriage, it would be his parents.

He parked his car in the back driveway and noticed his mom kneeling and pulling weeds in the flower garden. A rusty wheelbarrow, hose, and garden rake lay scattered about the yard. Brutus was sunning himself and gave a brief "stranger in the yard bark" and went back to sunbathing belly up.

"Hey, Mom."

"Oh, hi, sweetie. Could you please get that bag of peat moss and bring it here?"

"Sure thing. Um, you and Dad got a few minutes? I need to talk about something. It's kinda important."

"Okay, son, help me up here. These old bones aren't cooperating with the humid weather. I tell you what, getting old isn't for sissies!" she said brushing the dirt from her pants and took off her gloves.

Angus bent over took her hand and helped his mom up and they headed for the back door.

"Will, honey, you in there? Angus is here and wants to talk to us," his mom said removing her floppy sun hat.

"I'm in the den. Be right there."

"Angus, you and your father have a seat on the porch. I'll wash my hands and grab the sweet tea."

"That's sounds good. Thanks."

Angus and his dad each grabbed a wicker chair and sat under the sprawling oak tree covering the deck. The screen door creaked as his mom returned with the drinks and homemade sugar cookies.

"Son, you need to come by more often. I eat better when you're here," his dad said.

"Oh, stop complaining. Anyone can look at you and tell you ain't starvin," his mom said with a slight grin and swatted his dad's belly.

His dad snatched a second cookie. "What do you want to talk about?"

"Macey and I've been dating exclusively—going out for about three months now."

His mom smiled and nudged his dad under the table as they stole a glance at each other when Angus took a cookie from the Fiestaware tray. *They think they are so sly, I saw them look.*

"That's great news, Angus," his mom said. "I have always felt in my heart you two were meant to be together."

"Well…I'm thinking about proposing. But I'm not sure if I'm ready to settle down. How do you know? What happens if *the* perfect one comes along after I'm married? What then?"

"Well, son, if *the* perfect one comes along after you are married, you ignore her and run. You're married. It's as simple as that. Marriage is a lifetime commitment. Some days you will be glad you married, and others you won't *feel* like being married. You remember your commitment, realizing when your head hits the pillow, you made the right decision."

"Angus, honey, your dad is right. There'll be good days, great days, and hard days. Believe it or not, your dad and I have had a few tough times, but our commitment to God has always pulled us through."

She sighed and looked off into the sky and said, "I remember one of our biggest arguments happened when your father had gotten back from another long overseas business trip. Mr. Businessman here was used to delegating and having room service, fresh sheets and steak each night for dinner.

"I distinctly remember one argument when you kids were toddlers. I was exhausted, so I fixed *boxed* mac and cheese for dinner. The house had an 'I have toddlers, laundry to do, dogs, no time to clean, lived in look.' Your dad complained when he got home and asked, 'What have you been doing all day? The house is a wreck, you need time management skills.' I glared at him, then I

138

looked at you kids and said, 'You're a special kind of ungrateful, ain't ya? Here I am holding down the fort, and you're complaining? I do believe you'd complain if I hung you with a new rope.' He huffed off, came back and apologized a few minutes later. My point is the good days will outweigh the bad. Macey is the right one for you."

"Yes, she is. She knows you better than you know yourself. Macey's a sweet girl, we'd love to have her in the family in an official way," his dad added.

"Okay, I guess I'll start ring shopping. Please don't tell anyone, especially Clara. She never could keep a secret."

"Don't worry, son, we won't tell a soul," his mom said.

"Well, I guess I'd better get going." They gave Angus a hug, and his mom cleared the table as his dad walked him to the car.

He gave Angus another hug. "You sure you want to marry a Christian? You and Macey should have a long talk about that."

"Don't worry, Dad, I've worked this out. You've been traveling so much you didn't know we've been going to church together. Been attending a month straight now."

"Have you given your life over to God yet?"

"No, Dad, I haven't. I'm just trying to keep Macey happy. Not sure if I ever will."

"Son, you definitely need to rethink your decision. Marriage is hard enough with God at the center. Without God, it's even harder. You and Macey aren't teenagers. She's been through an awful lot in her short life, Angus.

You will need God as the foundation and center of your marriage."

"Sure, Dad, sure." Angus brushed aside his dad's comments and opened the car door.

"I love you, son. See you this weekend for lunch?"

"I'll be there. I love you too," Angus said and got in the car.

He leisurely cruised through town deciding if he should go to a local jewelry shop or the mall. "I guess I had better go to the next town. That way no one will see me going into a jewelry store and make the correct assumption."

He drove further on to Leesburg, a charming and historic town. A plethora of trendy boutiques, antique stores, and cozy coffee shops lined the streets. Ancient brick buildings, restaurants with cute patio tables in front, and flowers in large cement pots beautified the streets and corners. Tourists wearing sunglasses, coffee in hand, strolled by. He drove around the main square a few times and stopped at Stories to Tell Estate Pieces.

He parked out front. A burgundy awning covered the entrance offering shade to anyone who wanted to pause and view the array of knickknacks, books, and aged furniture neatly arranged in the display window. As he entered the shop, a teeny bell jingled as the dust particles danced and floated through the sun rays.

The shop owner was examining a coin. Lifting his head he said, "Hello, may I help you?"

The proprietor behind the counter dressed like someone in a time warp. He wore a baggy pair of pin-striped, high waist, cuffed pants, similar to the ones worn in the 1930s, and a knitted vest with a bow tie. In the far corner of the store near the satin curtained changing room stood a rack of vintage clothing. *Hmm must be where he gets his clothes.*

"Yes, sir, you can. I am searching for a uni-q ring. Uh, I meant a unique ring." He'd been around Macey so much now he was accentuating words like her.

"My name's Percival, I'm the owner," he extended his hand and said, "Well, you are in the right place. I have a large selection of antique rings. Do you know what you're looking for? Something for a sweetheart perhaps? An engagement ring, a wedding ring?"

"Actually, I need an engagement ring. If you don't mind, I'll look around and give you a holler when I see something that interests me."

"Okay, I'll be at the counter looking at more coins."

Angus walked around looking into the display cases. One case displayed chains and pocket watches of varying sizes, each with ornately carved dials, covers, and faces. To his left was a display packed with antique cufflinks and tie clips.

"Wow, I had no idea men's jewelry could be so expensive and ornate."

He took his time at the lady's ring case. There were emerald rings, sapphire rings, rings set in platinum, rings in yellow and white gold, rings with marquise cuts, oval cuts, and one and two carat gems in every stone imaginable. The vast display took him more than a few minutes to get through. Finally, he spotted a few perfect for Macey's personality.

"Percival, I found a few rings."

"Alrighty then." He looked up from another coin. "I'll be right over."

He walked across the red, well-worn antique diamond medallion Persian rug pulling out a gold chain attached to his vest pocket he found the right key. Angus pointed to a ring as Percival said, "You are a man of superb taste. This ring is indeed unique. Rarely, do I purchase a diamond such as this. Cushion cuts are hard to find, very scarce."

Percival jiggled the lock and carefully opened the glass case, placed the ring on a velvet cloth, and described the ring in detail.

"This piece is from the Edwardian period, 1900–1915."

"Oh." Angus cleared his throat. "That sounds very expensive."

"It might not be too bad. May I ask what's your price range?"

"Well, if possible, I'd like to keep it under $10,000. Do you have anything here in that range?"

"Yes, I do," he said and placed the ring back in the display case.

"I'm positive I have the perfect ring. It's also an Edwardian, I am certain you will appreciate its beauty. It's as you say very uni-q. I acquired it at an auction this past weekend. I haven't cleaned it yet, but you will see how beautiful it is despite that.

Percival fumbled for his keys. "Ah, yes. Here it is. It's a true beauty," he said and opened the drawer beneath the display case. He held the ring to the light and handed Angus the ring.

"It's not too often I possess two cushion cuts. It's a round pink peach diamond. The work during this time was exquisite. Notice the diamonds surrounding the center peach stone, they look like they are being held in place by lace. The craftsmanship of this period is extraordinary."

Angus held the ring to the light and admired the ring's clarity and quality. He turned it over in his palm, looking at how small it appeared in his large hands.

"You're right, this is a fine stone. What's it gonna set me back?"

"Well, a splendid ring such as this doesn't come along often. It's priced at $11,000."

Angus sighed, years of cheap living, used cars, and Ramen noodles, he managed to save quite a bit of money, but this ring would set him back. Still holding the ring, he paused and leaned over the case for a moment and said, "Well, sir, it's more than I can afford. Would you go $9,000?"

"I am afraid I can't let it go for that. Can you do $9,500?"

Angus nodded his head in agreement.

Percival walked over to the old National gold tone, push button cash register and rang up the sale. When he finished, he placed a hand written receipt in the striped velvet bag and stepped into the back to clean the ring. He emerged from the room polishing the ring with a jeweler's cloth, and then put the ring in a black velvet box, snapping the box shut. Smiling, he placed it in the bag and handed it to Angus.

Having the ring in the car made Angus nervous. It was practically burning a hole on the seat next to him, so with caution and speed, he hurried home. Once there, he changed his mind and decided he'd show Clara the ring and grabbed the ring box out of the bag. They often aggravated each other but remained close and confided in matters of importance. He shared most of his big life decisions with her, and she did the same.

Once at her place, he jumped out of the car. He burst through the back door and yelled, "Clara, Clara, I got to show you what I bought!"

"Hey, Angus, I am in the kitchen. Macey's here too," Clara said.

"Geez," he mumbled, stuffing the ring box in his cargo pants pocket. "That was close."

"I'm sorry, what'd you say? I wasn't paying attention," Clara asked, once again picking up the mess on the floor. "Brutus and Bullet have gorged themselves on the trash," she said as picking up the rancid leftover meatloaf and papers they had strewn across the kitchen floor. Macey sat at the table petting both dogs.

Angus scrunched his nose in disgust and said, "Geez, Macey, how can you let the dogs lick you on the lips?"

"Oh, Angus, for such a big guy you can be so delicate!" She rolled her eyes at him.

"Delicate ain't got a thing to do with it. I know where their tongues have been!"

"Oh, all right, down, Bullet, down, Brutus." Both obeyed and slinked away to lie on the sofa. "What were you going to show Clara?" Wrapping her arms around him, she stood and gave him a kiss.

"Nothing that can't wait. Hey, Clara, I promised Mom I'd check on Kolby. Want to ride over with Macey and me? Pastor saw Mom at the Piggly Wiggly and said he's stressing."

"Sure, give me a sec to change my shirt. I'll text Bryan on the way over. He can pick me up there. He's supposed to help Kolby assemble some of the baby paraphernalia."

Angus hurried out the door, and before the girls could reach the car, he stuffed the jewelry bag in the glove box and locked it. He opened the door for Macey, but not his sister.

"Hey, what am I chopped liver? No door for me?"

"Nope, sister pants, get in."

Angus hopped in the car, started the engine, and drove past the high school a few blocks away. School was letting out for the weekend, teens hovered in groups near the street—laughing, checking their cell phones and taking selfies—unconcerned about the traffic in the street. Angus, Macey, and Clara all laughed when one skinny boy, absorbed with his phone and not looking up, walked into a tree. A few blocks down the road, the elementary school also ended its day. School buses resembling giant yellow and black caterpillars lined the side of the street, some inching their way along the curb. Children carrying lunch boxes and backpacks ran amuck as moms tried to corral them, while chatting with other moms. *It's a nice small town kinda day.*

Macey and Clara chatted about babies, triplets, and other things. As they did, Angus' mind wandered to the ring. *Should I ask her tonight at dinner or take her out to*

CECE LIVELY

a special place? Nah, it needs to be special when I ask. Maybe something with Native American ties.

Lost in thought, he almost ran into the back of Bryan's car when he pulled into the long driveway in Kolby's and Tonya's backyard.

"Hey, man, watch out! Can't have an officer of the law in a fender bender *and* cause it," Bryan said. "Cop hitting a parked car wouldn't look good."

Angus abruptly stopped the car and looked at the house. Kolby and Tonya bought it two years ago. The stucco exterior and arched front porch entryway gave the bungalow a southwestern flare. Lots of work had been done to the place: new flooring, fresh paint, and new sod. Once the dumpy house in the neighborhood, now it looked very nice.

Not waiting for Angus to open their doors Macey and Clara hopped out and ran up the sidewalk and into the house. Angus heard Tonya holler as they walked in, "I'm back here in the bedroom, doing more resting."

***

Tonya sat on the bed, her feet dangling over it. She threw back the yellow and orange paisley coverlet with coordinating sheets and motioned for the girls to sit next to her on the bed.

"Girl, it's so dark in here," Clara said as she pulled up the shades and opened the curtains.

"I was watching happy ending movies. I must be having all boys. All I do is cry. I can't watch anything even remotely sad." She stared at her stomach. "Would

146

you look at this belly? I'm a beached whale! My belly is a road map of lines, so many red stretch marks. I'm so fat!"

"Oh, Tonya, you're having triplets. You're not fat, you're growing babies. Of course, you'll get big, but you will lose the weight chasing after the kiddies." Macey gave her a hug and rubbed Tonya's ample belly.

"I know, I'm trying not to get emotional. It's so hard. All I do is eat, use the bathroom, and cry." She flopped back on the bed, regretting that move as she struggled to sit back up.

"Okay, let's change the subject," Macey said as she took Tonya's hand, helping her to sit. "Have you decided on names yet?"

***

While the girls visited in Tonya's room, Angus motioned Bryan and Kolby to the corner, he turned his back to the hallway, and quickly showed them the ring, swearing each to secrecy.

"Man, that's a huge ring. I didn't know you two were serious," Bryan said.

Kolby let out a whistle. "Macey's going to love it. All of them will be drooling. You did good, bro."

As the girls talked, Kolby, Angus, and Bryan surveyed the front living room.

"Geez, wow, what happened here? Did a bomb go off?" Bryan asked astonished.

"Nah, this happens when you have to assemble *three* of everything," Kolby said.

Torn and opened boxes were strewn across the room. Stroller wheels were poking out of the sides of boxes, while canopies leaned against the only debris free area along the wall. Chunks of Styrofoam and its little spongy beads clung to one of the strollers and the flooring.

"I have never seen so many diapers in one place," Angus said while looking at an entire corner piled to the ceiling with boxes of disposable diapers. A stack of baby wipes almost reaching the top of the window teetered next to them. Next to those were mounds of crib bedding and blankets.

Kolby let out a whimper. "I don't know how I will do this. I get home from work, and I immediately try to put things together." He motioned with his hand. "Come and see the babies' room and the spare bedroom."

They all ambled down the hall. Angus and Bryan feigned fear and mimicked Kolby wringing their hands, wondering what lay behind those bedroom doors. Kolby opened the babies' room door, to reveal a room large enough to hold three cribs, three bassinets, and three dressers. They'd decorated each wall with a peel and stick on mural of pale blue and pink owls, and brown baby squirrels. Deer and foxes frolicked beneath the trees' fallen leaves. The one free wall had a wooden rocker nearby with another large tree with daisies beneath it.

Two doors down, Kolby opened the spare bedroom. They'd disassembled the bed and placed it against the far wall. The small room barely had space for the large changing table. Another rocker, more diapers, and a significant stack of baby bottles filled the room. A closet completed the cramped look, spilling over with blankets and infant clothing.

Angus exited the room stunned, no longer making fun of Kolby behind his back.

Kolby scratched his head, pacing back and forth in the living room. "My mom has sold her house. She finally says she has a reason to move closer. Where will I put her while she's here?"

Nervous, he ran his fingers through his hair. "There's no more room anywhere!" he said while rubbing the back of his neck. "I don't think I can handle this. Do you know what it's like to live with a crazy person the size of a small whale?"

Bryan gasped. "Shh, man, are you crazy? You can't say something like that around a pregnant woman."

"Too late. Last night I was talking to my mom, and I thought I was talking low so Tonya couldn't hear me, but she did. I said 'Mom, she's the size of a small whale,' and man did I ever catch it. Dude she cried for at least an hour, saying I hate her body and I think she is ugly. I'm still in the doghouse."

Kolby, bug eyed from lack of sleep, grabbed Angus by his shirt collar and said, "She craves gumballs mixed with instant potatoes! How gross is that? Last night as I prepared for bed, she was still sniffling about my comments…comments I made hours ago! After I got out of the shower, I hopped into bed and turned out the light. She rolled over and said I smelled and the odor of the soap I used made her sick. She *made* me shower again with no soap. She's crazy. I tell you, crazy. We were watching TV in bed, and she started crying over a flower commercial. I joked and said, 'Come out of there,' at her belly. I want my wife back,' and she started crying again."

He pushed aside the assortment of onesies and collapsed on the sofa muttering, "What am I going to do?"

"You'll be okay. I came over to help with assembling things while Clara keeps Tonya entertained," Bryan said.

"Guys, you have no idea how much I appreciate your help."

"It'll be okay. I can come on my next day off and help with stuff," Angus said, "But for now, I gotta go. Macey is cooking me and Pops dinner tonight at her place."

Angus popped his head in the bedroom and said, "Hey, Macey, let's get going. We need to go to Piggly Wiggly on the way and get your ingredients."

"Okay, Angus, I'm coming." She gave Tonya a hug and scurried out the door.

In the car, the talk centered on Kolby stressing.

"Macey, Kolby's a mess, He is so stressed."

"I bet. You should hear Tonya. She can't do anything except lay in bed. Says she's going nuts. Clara said she'd give her a pedicure since she can't reach her feet anymore."

They chuckled as Macey inched in closer to Angus. The Piggly Wiggly storefront advertised hamburgers, hot dogs, and chips on sale, none of which they were after tonight. He parked the car, opened her door, and grabbed an errant buggy as they entered the store.

Easy listening music played and someone called for a price check as they strolled through the produce aisle. Angus paused at a sample booth and took a sip of the energy drink he was offered.

"I am making Three Sisters Soup tonight. Have you ever had it?"

"No, can't say I have."

"Well, it's one of Pops' favorites. He's has been after me to make it. I need to get an acorn squash, canned pinto beans, and thyme. Grab the cornbread over there."

"Okay," Angus said as they browsed the produce department.

"Here, this squash looks good. It's organic, non-GMO," he said tossing it to her.

"How do you know that stuff?"

"Don't ask."

"Ah," Macey said with a knowing look on her face. "A yoga-pant, sport-bra, hippy-type old girlfriend?"

"Yah, it didn't last long. I grew tired of feeling guilty for everything: eating meat, wearing non organic clothes, buying food that wasn't fair trade, using too much electricity, and not reducing my carbon footprint. I felt guilty just breathing. She lasted almost a month, too much work."

While they were in the store, at least three little old ladies came up to Angus complaining about the noise levels at their corner lot houses where the stop signs were, saying the young hoodlums played music so loud their windows rattled. They went on about the trash on the streets, and graffiti on the buildings. Soon a few men came by, and they discussed guns and hunting. Angus replied kindly to each and had a soft answer to deflect the complaints.

"Wow, Angus, you certainly are a popular person in town. It's like being with a politician. I swear if those ladies had a baby in their arms, you'd have kissed it and posed for the cameras."

"Hey, I've gotta plan for my future when I run for sheriff, in twenty years!"

They cashed out, grabbed the bags, and headed toward the car.

As they left the store, Macey said, "I know what my superpower is."

"Huh?"

"My superpower is the ability to find the shortest line at checkout and have it take the longest."

Angus chuckled and helped Macey into the car. He then loaded the bags in the back seat and drove away.

"What's your superpower?" she asked.

Angus thought for a moment and said, "I guess it's the ability to handle multiple women at once without getting caught! But I think I've lost that superpower."

Macey smiled and poked Angus in the side. "Think? I should hope you've lost it."

As Angus rounded the corner, he saw Lucas in a loud, heated argument with the same woman.

"I wonder what he is up to, and who he's talking to?"

"Oh, that's his cousin, Kathy. I think she's a pharmacy assistant there."

"Well, they sure are having quite the discussion in public. Not sure what they could be talking about it must be important." He noticed they lowered their heads toward each other. "I'm gonna pull over and see if I can hear their discussion." He rolled his car to a stop near them.

Angus cursed and then apologized. "Sorry. I didn't mean to cuss in front of you. I can't get closer without being spotted. Whatever they're talking about, if it involves Lucas, it can't be good."

Kathy had a pinched annoyed look on her face as she stood near the door to the pharmacy smoking a cigarette. "Listen, Lucas, you can't keep coming here. I told you I won't give you any more information."

"If you don't, I'll let word get out that the pharmacy assistant takes recreational drugs," he threatened.

"You know that was years ago. 'Sides, I took a drug test when I got the job. You've got nothing on me Cuz."

"Well, no, but once I start rumors, you may have to take another drug test. How's the soda pop I gave you tasting? Good? You like it? Well, guess what?" He held a small brown glass vial filled with liquid in the air. "I slipped some oil in your drink, and I guarantee this contains enough THC to make you test positive. I can fix it so you test real soon."

Kathy swore and crushed the cigarette on the sidewalk with a vengeance. "Listen, this is the last time. I could lose my job, and I can't afford that. Jobs are hard enough to get here."

With mock concern he crossed one arm, put his hand to his chin with the other, and stared up at the sky. "Hmm, I'll have to think about it. Not! Whatcha got for me today?"

"Why are you being so greedy? I already gave you the names and addresses of seven people in the last two months who've had surgery and scripts for hydrocodone or some other narcotic."

"Let's just say Kelvin and I are making good side money."

"Kelvin? I mighta known. He's such a scum."

"Well, Cuz, ain't that the pot calling the kettle black. No pun intended." He laughed at his last comment.

"Huh?" she said puzzled.

"Pot, Kelvin's black, oh never mind. Don't be complaining. We've been generous with your cut."

"Lucas, I've got a bad feeling something awful will happen."

"Nah, you tell me who's had surgery and let me do all the worrying. I sneak in when they are all doped up, steal the meds, and no one is the wiser. Get a good price for them too."

"My boss said she is going to call Sheriff Rex tomorrow. She's catching on, too many people are losing their scripts and not able to find their meds."

"Ain't no one gonna get hurt, and I ain't been caught yet," he said then looked over his shoulder and leaned in closer.

Kathy glanced around. "All right, Mr. Richards is recuperating from double knee replacement. I overheard my boss's conversation. His daughter will get him home, and we'll deliver the meds to his place."

"What's the address?"

"353 Avenue A."

"I know where it is."

"His daughter said she will fix him a bite and make sure he takes his meds before she goes to work."

Excited, he danced about. "That's good. I've got plenty of time then. I love old people. We are raking in the dinero on all those knee and hip replacements and back surgeries!"

"Yah, well, you be careful and don't hurt anyone. My break is over, I gotta get back to work. You can come by on Wednesday with my cut."

Lucas said goodbye. Suspicious he looked around, and crossed the street.

"Well, looks like they finished." Angus waited a few minutes before he started the car and headed to Macey's place.

Chapter 15

He replied, "When evening comes, you say,
It will be fair weather, for the sky is red,
3 and in the morning, 'Today it will be stormy, for the sky is
red and overcast.' You know how to interpret the appearance
of the sky, but you cannot interpret the signs of the times.
Matthew 16:2–3 (NIV)

Angus pulled up to the curb. Hesitating, he held his breath then said, "Hey, um, before we go in, I need to talk to you about something. I don't want to have this discussion in front of Pops."

"Okay. What do you want to talk about?" she asked.

"Well, have we ever talked about your mom and dad? I mean what happened? Why did Pops start drinking?"

"I'm not sure where to begin. It's a long story, and it isn't pretty. It's not something I like to talk about." Her face flushed, and she slumped into her seat. "I'm sure you've heard the rumors around town," she said turning to meet his gaze.

"A few," he said clearing his throat.

"My dad wasn't around much and rarely after my mom died. From what Pops tells me, she was gorgeous and a mess. She got pregnant with me when she at sixteen and always found abusive men."

Looking out the car door window, Macey took a deep breath and recalled the day her mother died. "Funny what your brain remembers. I can picture her standing in the bathroom like it happened yesterday."

"Macey, shut the door! I'm half naked."

"Sorry, Momma. Momma, what's those purple marks on your arm and belly? Did you fall?"

"Um, well, sweetie, yes I did. Now shut the door."

"As a kid I thought nothing of it, but I pieced things together as I got older. She always dated losers. They'd get drunk, and she'd come home after a day or two banged and bruised. I guess that's why I date jerks."

"Hey, wait a minute!"

"Not you." She smiled. "I mean before you."

"My therapist says I date bad guys because I believe it's what I deserve. She says I am punishing myself because of the abortion. I imagine that is part of it, but mostly because it's how I grew up. Anyway, she kept dating losers and criminals. My grandparents were always arguing with her about her choice in men." She reached over and fiddled with the buttons on the car's dash.

"Pops and I got into horrible arguments over Lucas. He hates him. You don't know it, but he likes you. He told me the other day he is glad we are back together."

"Really? He sure has an odd way of liking someone."

"I must have seven or eight the day she died. One day my mom came home complaining of a horrible headache, probably from a hangover. I remember the old bathroom, the warped wooden floors, cracked mirror above the sink, and the nasty rusty water. The whole place was run down, like our lives." She gave a quiet sigh and continued, "I peeked in when she was bathing, and saw more bruising on her. She avoided looking at me, and hung her head, tears covered her face. I closed the door and said nothing. I went out to play, and a few hours later I heard my grandma's anguished scream. Mom had slit her wrists in the tub, and she found her dead."

A tear rolled down Macey's face which she quickly brushed away. "I wasn't sure what happened. I saw grandma on the floor rocking and moaning, her knees drawn up to chest, repeating the word, 'Why?' I'll forever see mom's hair floating peacefully among the bubbles in the water, her face submerged. Grandma tried to get me out of the bathroom, but I just stood there frozen. I asked grandma why the water was a pretty swirly red. She hugged me close and whispered, 'Get grandpa.'"

Macey turned abruptly to Angus, adding, "Did you know the suicide rate is extremely high among Native Americans compared to other groups and there's an eighty-nine percent increase among Native American women?"*

"No, sorry, I didn't know that. That's awful," he said reaching for a tissue in the glove box and pulling her closer to him.

"So that's how my grandparents ended up raising me. Every night Grandma would read me Bible stories. I loved the book of Esther. She'd call me beautiful and tell

* For details visit https://www.lakotalaw.org/news/2016-05-12/native-americans-facing-highest-suicide-rates

me God had great things for me. That I had a destiny. I had no clue what she meant. When my mom died, Pop's drinking got worse."

"Grandma and Pops argued non-stop over his drinking. She hated it. Late at night I'd hear them arguing, Pops cussing at her and grandma quoting scripture. That'd just make him madder, he'd storm off and she'd retreat to their bedroom crying and praying. It used to scare me, but I got used to it, I'd roll over and cover my head with the pillow drowning out their screams. I can remember how she'd take any money he got and hide it in her sock drawer, leaving him enough for beer so he wouldn't catch on. A year after my mom died, Grandma got cancer, and she died. I was so lonely. So, in a year and a half, Pops lost his daughter and his wife. Then his drinking really picked up."

"What made him stop drinking?"

"It was a combination of things. He said he saw a change in me when I became serious about church, plus he was thrilled when I broke up with Lucas. I told Pops I was changing and didn't want to be in an abusive relationship like Mom. And Pops has cirrhosis of the liver. I guess that got his attention and woke him up. One day, we were planting flowers and out of the blue he asked me, 'Macey, how do you do it? Keep having hope?' I told him it's a God thing. Jesus gives me hope and I have hope in seeing Grandma again. Pops is so odd. He smiled and shuffled back to the house to get another beer. That was the last time I saw him drink. He went to church with me that Sunday."

"Interesting. Do you remember I told you Lucas has a long rap sheet and a mean, unsavory reputation? Did he ever lay a hand on you?" Angus growled and gripped the steering wheel. "If he did, I'd be sure to teach him a lesson. I'd break his—"

"Relax, Angus." She smiled then nudged him. "No, he never laid a hand on me. I told him I was taking self-defense courses, and I'd kick his butt."

"Well, good to know. Remind me to not tick you off."

Macey chuckled. "I guess you'd better not."

"So, what about your dad? What happened to him?"

"He rarely came around once he got my mom pregnant, which was a good thing. The last I heard he did time for armed robbery. He was almost beaten to death for snitching. When I turned nine, he died. Later on, I found out he was shanked, whatever that is."

"A shank is a homemade knife, usually about this big." Angus held up his hands spreading them apart, "it's a piece of metal an inmate has sharpened and tightly wound with cloth or tape. If a person is shanked, it means someone has stabbed them. Prisoners make them and hide them from the guards for obvious reasons."

"So, it appears mister lawman is dating a woman with tons of skeletons in her closet."

"Well, the light is on in the closet and those skeletons can't rattle anymore. I guess we'd better get inside. I see Pops peeking out the window." Angus got out and opened her door. "Here, let me get those bags."

The rental house Macey shared with Pops was across the street from the town's only elementary school.

"Great house, Macey. I like the porch."

"Yah, we like it too. We've been here two weeks. Once I get everything out of storage, I plan on decorating the outside. Maybe nice floral cushions for the swing and a planter in the corner."

Angus opened the front door, and Macey shouted from the entryway.

"Hey, Pops, we're here."

"This is a lot nicer than the old beat-up trailer on the reservation. Nice hardwood floors," he said. A single blue denim sofa was in the living room and a blue checked recliner sat in the corner with a used trunk-style coffee table in front of it; there wasn't room for much else.

"Look, no cardboard over the windows or beer cans everywhere," she added.

"Beer cans?" Pops said. Grasping the bannister he slowly walked down the steps to greet them. "Macey, you know I don't drink anymore. I've been good since I started going to church."

"I know, Pops."

She turned with groceries in hand, whispering, "It's amazing what he can hear when he wants to. He must have worn his hearing aids today."

On the way to the kitchen Angus greeted Pops, and Pops smiled in response.

"Well, he's in a good mood. I didn't get the usual grunt this time."

"He should be in a good mood. I am making his favorite soup recipe my grandma used to make."

Angus surveyed the kitchen. It was small, sparse with decorations, with little room to move. Still Macey made good use of the space. A rolling cart in the corner held a blender, a stand-up mixer, and crock pot with extra pots and pans.

The window over the sink looked into the backyard, and Angus commented, "The view sure is better here than the reservation. You can see the park from the backyard."

"Pops and I have been trying to beautify the yard since we've been here. It's a nice rental. Last week we planted peonies and a lilac bush. This weekend we are hoping to plant perennials, maybe daisies, and salvia near the porch. Salvia is my favorite. I love the long purple spikes," she said as she unpacked the groceries.

"How's Pops liking it?"

"Well, he doesn't miss his friends, that's a good thing. All he did with them was drink."

"Hey, Pops, what happened to the can of corn I left on the counter?"

"Porn, what porn? What are you talking about? Angus you watching that porn?"

"No, Pops," she said in exasperation. "Corn, Pops, I said corn."

"Oh, a horn. I didn't hear a horn. Did you honk when you pulled in?"

"No, Pops." Macey walked over to him and cupping his face in her hands she calmly said, "Pops, corn, I said corn, not porn, not horn. What happened to the can of corn?"

"Oh, well, I put it back right where it should be. It's in the cupboard."

Macey looked over to see Angus wiping tears of laughter from his eyes.

Walking back to the kitchen she said, "Welcome to my world. Pops keeps things real interesting around here. You want to know what he said to your mom at the Piggly Wiggly?"

"Oh, lordy, what?"

"Well," she said, searching the cupboards for the errant can of corn. She opened another door, still no corn. "Your mom came over to our buggy and told me about your dad catching criticism for something at the church's board meeting. Wanna guess what Pops thought we were talking about?"

"Oh, do tell," Angus said drolly.

"Circumcision," she said, emphasizing each syllable.

He said, "Lordy, circumcision, why are you talking about that here? It's a cruel thing to do."

"Wow, I am truly speechless." Angus chuckled and leaned against the counter with his arms folded and legs crossed.

"Yup, he keeps things hopping. Geez, wherever did he put that corn?"

"Eureka!" Angus said as he got a soda out of the fridge, handing Macey the can of corn.

"Here, make yourself useful," Macey said handing a bag of vegetables to him. She saw him struggle to get the plastic bag open. "The scissors are in the drawer next to you."

"Thanks."

"Cut them—the cutting board is on the cart. Use the glass bowl to microwave them." She pointed to the clear glass bowl sitting on the shelf under the microwave cart.

"Hey, are you working tomorrow? I have a late appointment, so if you want to do anything it'll have to be after six," Macey said as she grabbed the pressure cooker. "Hand me that pot holder, these veggies are hot. Dinner won't be long now," she said as she set the table.

Angus paused for a moment and realized how blessed he was to have Macey back in his life, thinking what an idiot he'd been to leave town and her. He daydreamed as she stood near him in shorts and a snug pink T-shirt. He smiled as he admired her long, tanned legs.

He was startled from his pleasant thoughts when Pops strolled past him making little meow like farting sounds, pretending to be oblivious to what he did.

Macey laughed. "See what I mean? He does the most embarrassing things. Oh, well, I can only hope I'm as healthy as him at that age."

"Pee-yew," Angus said fanning his face.

Macey filled the bowls as Angus sliced the corn bread and placed it on the kitchen table.

"Hey, Pops, get back in here. It's time to eat," he said.

Pops moseyed to the kitchen. "Boy, say a blessing." He smacked Angus on the back of his head. "Don't just dig in. Be grateful for God's provision, say a prayer."

Angus groaned inwardly, then said a quick grace as they ate and discussed the day's events.

"It's been too quiet around here, hardly any calls, which is unusual for summertime. By now we should've had at least one shoplifting incident. The burglaries have picked up, but the bars have been quiet."

"That's always a good thing," Pops said.

"It is, but I can't help feeling things are brewing, and it won't be good," Angus said.

Pops finished his soup, excused himself, and left as Macey and Angus cleared the table.

"Hey, are these the old dishes my mom had? I remember the old Corelle gold flower pattern."

"Um hmm, she gave them to me a while back. This stuff is tough, lasts forever."

Angus washed as Macey dried and put the dishes away.

"Angus, I know Pops can be trying at times, but I am so proud of him. It's been months since he had a drink. He's really absorbing pastor's sermons, and he's reading his Bible every chance he gets; says he is making up for lost time. It's amazing. Late last night, I got myself a glass of water, and I heard a noise coming from his bedroom. I peeked in his room and he's praying and praising God in his sleep! His arms were raised, and he was singing in his native tongue. It gave me goosebumps."

"Wow, that's amazing." Not wanting to have a conversation involving God, he changed the subject. "Hey, let's go out tomorrow. Maybe a hike in the woods nearby? Sound good? I can pick up some snacks at the store, and we can have a picnic," he said rubbing the ring box in his pants pocket.

"That'd be nice," she said inching closer to him.

Angus tossed the damp dish towel on the counter as the two walked to the living room. "You know next time is my turn to pick the movie. These chick flicks are so boring."

"Well, I can't say I find your crash and burn stuff interesting either, but here we are," she said plopping down on the sofa next to Angus.

Pops shuffled from the bathroom, tilted his head, raised his eyebrows above his glasses, and then sat down between them.

Macey crossed her arms and sighed heavily, "Really?" Then motioning with her head, she added, "Uh, the recliner is available."

"I can see the TV better from here. You know how bad my eyes are."

Angus mouthed over Pops' shoulder, looked at Macey and said, "It's okay. My mind wasn't on the movie anyway."

He sat next to Pops, the ring burning a hole in his pocket as he imagined life with her. A woman cried in the movie, and his mind wandered to them growing old together. Funny, he imagined guys didn't do this sort of thing, but he found himself doing this more and more.

"Finally! I can't believe I wasted an hour and a half of my life watching that stupid sappy movie." Before heading to his bedroom, Pops grumbled and stretched, looked at his watch and said, "Would you look at the time, it's 10:30, time for these old bones to go to bed."

"I agree, Pops, it was a stupid movie, and you're right. I gotta go. We both have work in the morning."

Macey stood and walked Angus to the door; they waited until Pop's was out of sight before they said good-night. *She is so tiny and beautiful.* Resting her head on his chest she inhaled the scent of his cologne. He grinned then stooped down and cradled her in his arms as they kissed. His heart pounded and he felt her knees weaken as she sighed, holding him closer.

After a few minutes Pops emerged, wandered into the living room in search of his eyeglasses, cleared his throat, and frowned saying, "Good night, Angus."

He took the cue. "Good night. I'll see you tomorrow. Call me when you are ready, and I'll pick you up."

"Okay," Macey said as she shut the door.

Angus paused at the front door long enough to hear Macey shout, "Pops, you really didn't have to do that. I *am* an adult. Hey, silly old man, I know you can hear me." She laughed.

Angus walked to his car, got in, and drove through town. A dog barked and crickets chirped, he could see silhouettes in the windows above the stores. "Sure is a different place at night, quiet, the soft glow of streetlights, the occasional cat crossing the street, it's so serene," he said to no one in particular.

These would be the last few tranquil days for a long while. For Angus was unaware the enemy of his soul had him in his crosshairs.

Chapter 16

When you pass through the waters,
I will be with you;
and when you pass through the rivers,
they will not sweep over you.
When you walk through the fire,
you will not be burned;
the flames will not set you ablaze. Isaiah 43:2 (NIV)

Angus showered and got ready for work. He walked into the kitchen and picked up the ring box he'd left on the counter. Opening it, he held the ring to the light, admired it for a moment, snapped the box shut and placed it back on the counter. He perused the vacant fridge for something to eat, finding nothing except moldy tuna and cheese. He shut the fridge door, his stomach still growling, "Well, today is the day, its official. As of this evening I am off the market."

He ran his fingers through his hair. *With Macey by my side I can conquer the world or at least Riverside.* Smiling, he poured a cup of coffee into his travel mug, grabbed the keys, headed out the door, and bounded down the steps two at a time to his car.

Angus started the engine, the car lurched and then sputtered. He leaned back against the seat and tried again.

"Ah, man, not today! I can't believe this is happening," he grumbled, lifted the hood and swore when he banged his head on it. He meant to take the Bronco for service but hadn't. *Probably the starter.* He shut the hood and trudged up the steps, dialing Sherman's number.

"Hey, Sher, can you give me a ride to work? I think the starter is out on my car. I'd walk, but the sky is all crazy looking. One side is sunny, and the other side looks like one hellacious storm is brewing."

"Sure. Be there in a few."

"I really need to clean," Angus said staring at the sink full of dirty dishes, boxes of opened cereal, and half-eaten toast. A carton of sour milk was stinking up the trash. He stared at the clipped toenails on the end table, remembering how disgusted Clara and his mom were by this peculiar habit he'd picked up from his dad.

"I'd better do some kissing up to Mom. Maybe she'd come and clean." Then he remembered he'd have to listen to her lecture on the state of the place. He opted to do it himself.

He went to the closet, pushed aside the pile of muddy shoes and sports equipment on the floor, grabbed the ancient Kirby, and plugged it in. If he hurried, he could vacuum up the toenails on the end table, before anyone, especially Macey saw them.

He heard Sher pull in and the car horn blaring outside. He stuck his head out the window, turned off the vacuum and hollered, "Be right there."

Grabbing the keys again, he locked his door and headed to the squad car.

"I really appreciate you picking me up."

"Sure, no worries." She sipped her coffee and ate a peanut log donut.

"These are awesome. Have you tried one from the new bakery, The Kitchen Sink, on the square?"

He buckled in and replied, "Not yet."

"If you want one, there's another in there." She pushed the box toward him.

"Thanks," he said as they continued small talk on the way to the station.

***

"Hey, Pops, I will be home late tonight. I'm going on a picnic with Angus."

Macey grabbed the blueberry pie she made earlier and headed out the door.

"Okay, honey, see you later on tonight. I'll wait up for you."

"No need to do that," she said and grabbed her rain-coat and got into her dog grooming van. She had to admit, the local automotive shop did a marvelous job revamping the used van she bought a few months ago for her business. The repair shop removed the van's rusted doors and pulled out the dents, then painted pink and blue stripes on it, running the length of the van. The sliding door had the shop's logo, Pawsome Grooming, complete with silhouettes of dogs and cats on each side. The vehicle's bright colors and bold lettering attracted business. It cost a small fortune but was worth the investment.

Macey gave Clara call. "Hey, Angus has been acting kinda weird lately, so I made him his favorite blueberry pie. I'll drop it off and be right there."

"Okay. If any clients come by, I'll let them know. You be careful, it looks there's a gully washer coming," Clara said.

"Okay, thanks." Macey looked out the windshield at the sky. *Wow, the weather forecaster wasn't kidding. The temperature has dropped, and those clouds. Odd how the town's half sunny and half stormy. I wonder if there's a tornado watch.*

Macey drove a few more blocks to the square and headed to Angus' place, hoping to catch him at home. *Good, his car is still in the drive.* Her heart raced, like it always did in anticipation of seeing him. She got out and grabbed the pie on the passenger seat.

"Hello Grammie, how are you doing?" Macey said as Grammie slowly bent over and picked up the stray Gazette paper on the side porch.

"Morning, Miss Macey." Grammie smiled.

***

After another rough night of tossing and turning, Belissa got out of bed.

"May as well get up and go for a jog, before it rains…again." She threw back the sheets and looked out her bedroom window.

Yawning, she walked to the bathroom, and remarked, "Hmm, what to do with my hair today? Updo? Headband?" She primped, styled, and teased her hair for a long while, and once satisfied said, "No reason a girl can't look good working out." Admiring her hair, she patted her tiny sports bra, and turned to view her sleek figure in the full-length mirror on the back of her bathroom door.

Turning, she smiled and congratulated herself on the tight yoga pants that hugged her every curve and the barely there sports bra that matched the spider web print on the pants. "Girl, you look good enough to eat!"

Belissa snatched a cold water bottle from the otherwise empty fridge, turned and locked the door, and went down the steps. She paused for a moment at the corner curb, deciding what direction to take.

"I think I'll go by Angus' place and see what he is up to." She placed her ear buds in and began her jog to the crashing music of her favorite heavy metal CD. She looked and crossed the street as two teens walked past her and whistled. As a reward for their attention, she stretched and touched her toes ever so deliberately, then winked and waved as she continued her jog.

She paused when she rounded the corner to see Angus get in the squad car and drive off with a woman.

"Hmm, I wonder if I can find out what he is up to?" she said as she waited for them to leave.

Once they were out of sight, she went to his mailbox. "I know it's here," she muttered as she fumbled with the bottom of the mailbox and grabbed the spare apartment key he had magnetized to the bottom.

"Got it!" She scurried up the steps, then opened and shut the door quickly. "What a mess." She swore as she tripped over the wadded up vacuum cord. Staring at the dirty kitchen, she fanned her face for fresh air. She spotted the ring box on the counter and grasped the counter to steady herself and let out a gasp.

"Oh no! He wouldn't!" Reaching for the box she opened then snapped it shut when she heard a car pull into the driveway. Running to the couch she peered through the blinds and saw Macey pulling in and talking to Grammie. Belissa stood next to the window out of sight, but close enough to hear every word through the window blinds.

"Hello Grammie, is Angus home? I made him a pie, and I wanted to put it in his icebox for our picnic tonight."

"Oh, Macey, what a beautiful pie. I might sneak up and get a piece myself." Grammie laughed.

"Um, Grammie, I don't mean to cut you short, but it looks like more rain is coming."

"I think you're right. The sky looks positively pregnant with rain!"

"Well, I'd better hurry in before the sky gives birth!"

"All right, honey, let me get you the key and you can go on in." Grammie shuffled off to the house in her robe and slippers.

At first, Belissa wanted to trash his place but thought better. Her lips tightened, and she reached for something, anything to throw. *Control yourself girl.* She twirled her hair with her fingers and grinned, snapping her fingers as a wicked smile crept across her face. "I'll teach her a lesson she'll never, ever forget!"

Belissa thought quickly and ran to the bedroom. She barely had enough time to muss up her hair, pull off her bra, and put on Angus' robe. She ran to the bathroom and splashed water on her face as she heard Macey come up the steps. The door unlocked. *He gave her a key!*

Macey balanced the pie as she opened the door to Angus' apartment. She heard a door shut. "Hello, is somebody here?"

"Oh, Angus, stop that!" Belissa said loud enough for Macey to hear. "Hold on a minute, honey. I'll be right back."

A barefoot and perspiring Belissa came down the hall barefoot, with her pants rolled up under the robe and her hair in disarray. Angus' old flannel robe was strategically pulled down exposing a bare shoulder.

Macey's eyes widened. Shocked, she dropped the pie—blueberries and glass splattered across the tile leaving swirls of indigo colored sticky goo splattered across the floor. She ran out the door and down the steps. "No, no, it can't be true!"

She yanked open the van door and got behind the wheel. Pounding the steering wheel, she screamed, "Now I know why you have been acting so weird. I can't believe you went back to her, *her*! I should've known. How could I have been so stupid? You'll never hurt me again Angus Connors!" Macey jerked the van into reverse almost hitting old Houdini as she sped down the street in tears.

"Well, well, well, bless her little pea pickin' heart. I upset little miss perfect. Hah!" Belissa snickered. Returning to the bedroom, she put her designer running shoes and sports bra back on, and flung the robe in the corner where she found it.

At the bedroom mirror she pretended being at an awards show. With microphone in hand, she said, "Mrs. Baker, what a truly stellar performance. Is there anything you would like to say?"

"Why, thank you ever so much," she gushed. "I have been given a great talent." Waving a faux trophy in the air she bowed. Then putting her hands to her face in a gross caricature of Macey, she mimicked and sneered, "No, No, it can't be!"

Flopping on the bed, she congratulated herself. "I showed you, didn't I? I told you not to dump me." Gleeful, Belissa rolled across the bed several times giggling as she did so. After a minute, tears of conflict and regret formed, her chin quivered as a quiet sob escaped. Macey had not brought her purposeful pain, ever. For a moment remorse set in, but she pushed it aside stuffing it inside her heart. She walked to the bathroom to tidy up her hair. "Perfect," she said and left the apartment.

With deliberation she went down the steps. "If I can't have him"—another step—"then you"—step—"surely can't," she said, repeating the words at each footfall. At the mailbox she cracked, "Job well done," and replaced the key.

At the end of the drive, she did a few stretches knowing Willard watched in admiration. Putting the earbuds back in, and before turning up the volume she heard Grammie.

"What you looking at, old man? Put your eyes back in your head."

***

Activity picked up at the station. Bad weather had a way of increasing police calls.

"Sheriff, you need to go to the new drugstore. Just got a call from the pharmacist," Jean said as she rose from the battered metal green desk and handed Rex her notes. "Sonya wants to talk to you about some prescriptions coming up missing? Not sure what that means, she sounded pretty frustrated."

"I got another call, another break-in." Rex handed the paper to Angus. "Here, you and Sherman check this out and let me know what's going on." He grabbed his cowboy hat and headed out the door.

Sherman drove the squad car to the pharmacy and pulled in behind the building next to the big blue trash dumpster. Getting out of the cruiser, Angus radioed in that they'd arrived.

"Glad to see you." Sonja the pharmacist saw them pull in and went to the back door. "Let's go in the store-room where we can talk privately. Something is up. In the last few weeks I've had five customers come in and say they can't find their brand-new prescriptions they had filled the same day they returned home from surgery. The scripts are for either Hydrocodone or OxyContin. Each had a two-week supply, now either they're extremely absentminded or something else is going on."

"Do you have the names and addresses of these folks?" Angus asked.

"Sure do."

Sonja came back and read the addresses as Sherman wrote them down.

While writing, she glanced from her note pad at Angus with a knowing look.

"Thank you for letting us know." Sher tucked the notepad in her front pocket.

"We'll check into this, and we'll talk with each person. Thank you for keeping us informed," Angus said.

Outside Sherman said, "Can you believe it's the same list of break-ins reported at the station?" She got behind the wheel.

"Yah, the weird thing is the stuff taken was insignificant: change off the dresser, food from the freezer, and a necklace were missing. Weird, just weird. Looks as if they were also taking the drugs. I guess no one noticed scripts were missing until after our reports. Sher, swing by County. Let's check if any more surgeries are coming up."

"Good idea. Maybe we can get a lead on the next hit."

"Yah, that's what I was thinking. Wow, look at those clouds, didn't Jean say we're in a flash flood watch? It's gonna be a bad storm," he said looking out the window at the roiling purple and blue clouds.

As Angus spoke, the clouds opened, and a torrent of water ripped from the clouds so hard the wipers couldn't keep up. They pulled under an overpass to wait for the deluge to subside.

Angus' cell phone rang. He groaned. "Quit calling me, Belissa. I'm not gonna pickup. You crazy B. Leave a message."

It was still raining hard when they heard Jean's voice crackle over the radio. "Sher, Angus, you there? Pick up!"

Angus grabbed the radio. "Jean, what ya got?"

"It's Macey. She's at the bridge. Just got a call from someone, she's about to jump."

"What the?" Angus let out an expletive as Sherman floored the car and headed to the bridge.

Racing through two of the town's three stop lights, the car screeched to a halt at the bridge, and Sherman turned off the siren. Angus unbuckled his seatbelt, then ran to the bridge in the driving rain.

He tried to remain calm. Bewildered, with his hands outstretched, he asked, "Macey, Macey, honey, what are you doing?"

"Don't call me honey," she screamed at him through the rain as the thunder rolled overhead.

He approached her with caution. "Macey, honey, step away from the rail. Please don't do this."

"I said don't call me honey!" she yelled above the thunder, brushing wet hair out of her eyes.

He could tell she had been crying hard. Her whole face was swollen and red.

"Macey, please, this is dangerous. Come away from the rail." Wind gusts bent the trees, one limb snapped and flew across the bridge. The rain came down in sheets sideways, Angus had to shield his eyes from the rain in order to see Macey.

The sun raced behind the clouds, as they continued to pour rain. Angus had to remove his sunglasses to see her.

"No! I can't let you hurt me anymore."

"What are you talking about? Suicide is permanent and whatever is going on is temporary."

She walked closer to the rail.

"Macey, don't!" Angus hollered as she stepped up onto the rail, barely holding on to the bridge trestle.

"Macey, please," he pleaded and stepped closer. "Don't do this."

She turned, and through the rain she shouted goodbye and jumped into the swirling, muddy Rivanna River.

Angus rushed forward looking down, the last thing he saw were strands of long black hair churning in the furious current below.

"Get the rope. Sher, get the rope. Hurry!" Angus said as he ran downhill toward the slippery embankment. He slid and tried to keep himself upright in the mud and the rain. Sherman tossed the rope. Angus dropped his holster on the grass, and tied the rope around his waist as Sherman anchored it to an old oak tree nearby, and then he plunged into the fuming, raging river.

The water was an inch or two above his waist, rushing past him. He struggled to see her in the downpour, sputtering as the rain washed over his face. He thought he spotted her.

Pointing to the bridge piling, Sherman screamed, "She's over there!" as another peal of thunder shook the ground.

"Oh, God, no!" Angus cried as he made his way to her. He hit a deep spot where the water approached his shoulders.

The swift dark water rushed past him, if it weren't for the rope around his waist he would have drowned. He went under twice but reemerged.

"Macey, honey, no!"

She was face down in the river, her head below water. Trash that accumulated from the rain was entangled in her hair. He fought the current to remove her from the debris around the bridge piling. Gasping for breath in the downpour he turned her over and noticed the huge cut on her head. Profuse blood ran down her face and onto her shirt, turning it pink.

"Stay with me, Macey! Stay with me, Macey!" he cried out, fighting the current, trying to hurry back to the shore.

He placed her on the soggy ground, kneeling beside her, moaning, "No, God. No. Please, no!" he said brushing her hair from her face.

Sherman grabbed Macey and rolled her over on her back. She screamed at Angus as she wiped the rain from her eyes, "Get it together if you want her to live. I've radioed an ambulance. We need to start resuscitation." She started CPR, when she turned Macey on her side, water trickled out of her mouth.

She went into medic mode, and placed her fingers in Macey's jaw below her ears, jutting the jaw forward. Leaning in, she strained to hear a breath against the howling wind and rain. There was no chest movement. Macey wasn't breathing.

She cleared her airway and barked at Angus, "Check for a pulse."

He shook himself came to his senses and checked. "No pulse, Sher."

She began compressions as Angus counted, "One, two, three." When he reached thirty, she gave Macey two deep breaths.

She coughed just as the EMS attendant arrived with the stretcher. They were unable to maneuver around the mud and rocks, so Angus carried Macey to them, his shoes creating suction with each step. He fell to his knees in the mud twice.

He placed her on the gurney and noticed the head wound was worse than he first thought.

By now, Macey had a raccoon look around her eyes, and large red marks on her face and arms, her jaw line was swelling fast. Angus saw clear fluid leaking from her nose, her ears. Each were definite signs of severe head trauma. Her body convulsed, and her back stiffened as her eyes rolled back in her head. He saw vast amounts of blood flowing down her neck, and he was afraid her skull was fractured. Looking away he knew she might not make it.

The EMTs shut the doors and the ambulance raced to the hospital, sirens blaring.

He trudged to the cruiser and slouched in the seat holding his head. "I just don't get it. I was going to propose to her tonight. Why? Why did she jump?" They buckled in. Sherman handed Angus his service weapon and followed the ambulance to the hospital.

Chapter 17

Do not be afraid, for I am with you;
Isaiah 43:5 (NIV)

The ambulance pulled through to the emergency entrance canopy. The paramedics opened the doors and rushed Macey into the ER.

Angus raced to Macey's side. He slipped and grabbed the rail leaving streaks of mud on the floor. He steadied himself and heard the ER doctor say, "Put her in the first bay. What's her current BP? What happened?"

"Mid-twenties, female, head injury, BP is low, 70 over 50. Looks like we have cerebral edema," one EMT said catching his breath. "Suicide attempt. She hit her head on a bridge piling, been underwater for about three minutes. Noticed clear fluids from the nose and ear, not looking good, doc."

A harried nurse came running in as the doctor ordered, "Let's start an IV and push fluids in her to try to get her BP normal and keep it from falling. Call imaging and get a CT scan STAT. We need to find the source of the swelling and its extent. She'll need a neuro's expertise. Call the other area trauma units and see if anyone has

a neurosurgeon who can get here and treat her ASAP."
Another nurse entered the ER bay. "On the count of three
let's lift her. One, two, three," the doctor said.

Angus overheard the conversation, while pacing the
ER corridor in his waterlogged boots. The sterile smell
of the hospital gagged him, and he covered his mouth.
Come on get it together, you're a cop. He composed
himself and grabbed his phone. Frustrated, he repeatedly
pressed numbers, but the screen was blank. Slamming it
on the counter, he said, "Water must have destroyed it."
His boots squished as he hurried to the nurses' station to
use the desk phone.

"Mom, Mom, come on Mom, pick up," he cried
frantically into the receiver as it rang on the other end.
"Mom, you there? Listen, get to County fast! It's Macey.
She jumped off the bridge and—"

"What? She did what? Why?" his mom stammered.

"She jumped and has a severe head injury. Wait, let
me see what the doctor is saying."

"Okay," the doctor said, looking at the nurse, "Any
luck finding a neurosurgeon?"

The nurse shook her head no.

"Then find one who can walk me through an external
ventriculostomy. We need to put a tube in her to drain the
cerebrospinal fluid and relieve the pressure on her skull.
Let's get moving team. We don't have much time."

"Mom, they are talking about putting a stent in
Macey's brain. It looks…She jumped and was underwater for a few minutes. I had to go into the river and get
her out." He turned and pressed his forehead against the
wall and cried.

"I'm sorry, son, we are on our way." Her voice quivered, and she struggled for words. "I-I-I just don't know what to say. I'll stop by and pick up Pops, and call Pastor and Clara on the way and get her on the prayer chain. We'll be there as fast as we can."

"Thanks, Mom. I don't think she's going to make it. I really don't."

"It's okay, son. God is in control."

"How can you say that?" he asked, hanging up the phone before she could reply.

Before leaving the house, she called Clara's work. "Sweetie, you need to get to County ASAP. It's Macey," and proceeded to fill her in.

Dogs were barking in the background and Clara had to cup her hand to the phone to hear her mom. "What's happened to Macey?"

"She jumped."

"Wait, I couldn't hear you. Did you say she jumped?"

"Yes, and Angus doesn't know if she'll pull through. Pray, Clara, pray, real hard."

Clara turned to her veterinary assistant, briefed her on Macey and had her reschedule the days remaining appointments. She jumped in her car and raced to the hospital.

Angus was leaning against the banister for strength when Sherman ran into the ER out of breath.

"Hey, Jean called. There's a disturbance at Joey's BBQ. What a time for Mark to go on vacation. I can't believe this day. Rex said to take this call. He can't get there in time. I hate to do this to you, but we gotta go, Angus."

Angus' boots squished out water and left mud tracks in the hall when he and Sherman ran to the squad car. Sirens pierced the air as they headed to Joey's BBQ.

***

"Belissa, let me in," Lucas said, letting out a string of swear words while banging on her apartment door. "Come on, it's pouring out here. I'm getting soaked."

"Hold on, I'm coming!" She opened the door and let him in. "What's up? I was in the bathroom doing my hair." She shouted above the music playing from her iPhone.

"You spend way too much time on your hair. It's really coming down out there. Listen, I want to talk with you about Angus. Wait," he said as his ringtone played *Bad to The Bone*, "it's my brother Chokker."

"What's up, bro?"

He looked at Belissa and lowered his voice as he walked to the hallway so she couldn't hear the conversation. "Yah, man, I got an idea for Angus. I wanna get that," he said, and let loose more expletives. "Listen, the next house we break into, we gotta figure out a way to get him. He's a real piece of—" Frustrated with his brother, Lucas' voice grew tense as he cursed loudly at him. "Shut up, would ya? Kathy saw Angus and Sherman come into the pharmacy today. They are onto us. I've got one more house tonight, and then we gotta lay low for a while. What? You idiot! Why? Didn't you hear me? Listen, we can set him up. I got a gun. I know, I know. I told Kathy no one would get hurt, but this is a perfect opportunity."

Belissa cupped her hand over the phone and whispered, "Angus, please pick up. I know you don't want to talk to me, but this is important. I don't have much time. Lucas and his brother are planning something." Looking up she saw Lucas glaring at her.

"Hey!" Lucas shouted and rushed at her, ending his call. "What the hell? What do you think you're doing?" he roared and slapped the phone from her hands, causing it to sail across the room, landing near the apartment door.

"Warning lover boy? You think you can mess with me?" He sneered and grabbed her by the throat, pushing her into a corner. He backhanded her hard across the face with his calloused, oil stained hand.

"Please, Lucas, don't. I didn't mean it. It was nothing." She cried as she held her cheek. Her heart raced. She'd heard enough stories concerning Lucas and knew her life was in danger. Flinching as he raised his hand to punch her again, she desperately looked around for anything to defend herself. She grabbed a lamp, but he knocked from her hands, sending it crashing to the floor, spraying glass everywhere.

Lucas got in her face, and she could feel the heat of his breath. He twisted his head and sneered. "Sure, I'll stop! What's that? Trying to reach for something?" He screamed more expletives above the pounding music and wrenched her arm backwards, causing her to shriek in agony. Between the loud music and the crowd at Joey's cheering their favorite football team, no one heard Belissa's screams as he beat her mercilessly.

She fell to the ground.

"You stupid, little—" He kicked her in the ribs with his steel toed boots. "I'll teach you to mess with me!" He repeatedly kicked her, then he picked up her limp body and threw her against the wall so hard her body left an indent in the drywall. He held her up as she slumped from the beating, moaning. He punched her in the nose, causing blood to spurt. "You think you can protect yourself with your potions and spells? Ha! Bless your little pea pickin heart." He laughed, tilted his head, sneered and said, "You really have no idea who you are messing with, do you?"

Squinting through her swollen eyes, she saw demons slithering along the walls, imps on Lucas' shoulder encouraging him.

"Stupid, poor Belissa, let's see if lover boy can come to your rescue now," he said mocking her and banging her head into the wall. No longer able to endure the pain she collapsed. He pushed up against the wall for one last punch. Doing so caused her hair piece fall to the floor, exposing her short hair and bald patches. "What the? Aw, too bad and you just did your hair."

He gave her another kick, and for good measure, he stomped on her belly. She moaned and managed to mumble the word stop. He stood back as she lay on the living room floor.

"Damn good work. You'll never mess with me again." He straightened his dirty and bloodied wife beater T-shirt, grabbed a beer, popped the top, and took a long chug. Smirking, he crossed his arms and admired his work. He gave a loud belch and poured the remaining beer over her. Then he gave her another kick to make sure she wasn't responsive and left, not bothering to shut the door.

Belissa came to a few minutes later. With great effort, she crawled to her cell phone Lucas had flung from her hand when he first hit her. She dialed 911.

"911 operator, what is your emergency?"

"Help me. Please, hurry," were the last words she managed to mumble through her broken jaw as blood filled her mouth and lungs.

***

"Holy crap, what is going on today? Is it a blue moon, full moon?" Sherman asked as she sped down the road tires squealing.

"Let's get there. I'll check out the bar first and if needed do a quick walk around," Angus said. An ocean of angry charcoal clouds canvassed the sky. The metallic smell of lightning filled the air as thunder boomed and the ground shuddered.

The squad car screeched to a stop in front of Joey's. Angus radioed Jean. "10-23, arrived at scene." He flung the door open and stepped into a huge puddle, further waterlogging his soggy boots. "Well, that's great, just great."

They entered the bar, it had a lousy reputation and they were surprised when all seemed relatively calm, at least for a bar.

Sherman walked in the bar. "Someone here call 911?" she shouted above the noise and looked around.

Joey shook his head no and continued to draw a draft beer for a customer at the bar. "Nah, man, nothing happening here. Prank call maybe?"

"I don't have a good feeling. Something's not right, Sher. Let's do a walk around."

They walked out. Sherman looked up at Belissa's place.

Her door was open. "Uh oh, Angus." She motioned with her head toward Belissa's open door as it banged in the wind.

With their hands on their side arms they walked up the steps.

"Holy, mother of God," Sherman said. "Look at her! I don't think she's alive."

"Belissa!" Angus tapped his shoulder radio. "Jean, get an ambulance here to Joey's ASAP. Looks like a 10-36, assault." He surveyed the apartment—it looked like a bomb went off, end tables overturned, lamps on the floor, and beer cans scattered throughout. A stark bloody hand print was smeared on the wall next to Belissa.

"Geez, Sher, what happened to her? Is she even alive? Does she have a pulse?"

Sher retrieved a pair of gloves from her pocket and put them on. "Her pulse is weak and irregular, forty at best. Don't move her until we have to. She's taken quite a beating."

The shriek of the ambulance barely registered above the thunderstorm. The same EMTs from Macey's jump raced up the steps and into the room carrying their first ALS, advanced life support bag.

"Wow, she's pretty bad. Angus, a little help here? On the count of three, let's lift her on the gurney and get her down to the hospital."

A crowd from the bar and neighborhood formed at the bottom of the steps. The EMTs placed Belissa on the gurney and rolled her through the group, as people took pictures and called their friends.

"Unbelievable! Do you people have no shame? Pictures? Really?" Sherman said, glaring at the crowd, shaking her head in disgust.

Belissa was loaded into the ambulance as Sherman and Angus followed it to County.

"Man, Sher, she looks awful. I haven't seen a beating like that ever, and I've seen a lot, a lot," Angus said as they followed the ambulance.

His stomach lurched from the stress of the day. "Hey, can I use your phone? I need to call my mom, she's friends with Belissa's mother."

She handed him her phone. "Yah, sure." She tried to offer words of reassurance but had none.

"Mom, you need to get a hold of Belissa's mother. Someone has beaten her, and it's severe."

"What? Oh, lordy! I'll get a hold of Betty and add Belissa to the prayer chain. Sweet Jesus, what's happening?"

"Mom, I'll meet you at the hospital."

Once inside, Angus heard the paramedic say as they burst through the glass ER doors, "Looks like an assault. Got a female, mid-twenties. BP is fifty-five over thirty. Severe head trauma, possible broken nose, jaw, ribs, and a fractured cheekbone. Unresponsive."

The doctor began working on Belissa and instructed the team, "We need X-rays, and CT scan, now. There's no way we can determine the extent of her injuries until we get the results. Let's save a life tonight."

Belissa was prepped and taken to imaging.

Angus watched the doctor apprise Belissa's mom of her injuries. His dad and mom stood next to her. His dad caught Betty before she fainted, crying out, "Oh, Jesus, sweet Jesus!"

Angus checked on Macey. He peered into her room. She lay on the bed motionless, tubes and IV's in her arms, oxygen mask attached, and bandages around her head. He could hear the quiet beep of the vital monitors in the corner.

He saw Pops. "How is she?""

"It's not good. It's touch and go. I felt this was coming, last night I dreamed and saw the Indian symbol for death, a woman stick figure upside down. Then I saw a great buffalo, an eagle, and a brilliant cross. God is telling me she will not die. What the enemy has meant for death, God will turn to life. In my culture the great buffalo means strength and provision, and God will provide during this difficult time. And the eagle assures me that as he soars above, my prayers are being carried to God. She has great strength. I will continue to war with the demons, and God will prevail."

"I believe you, Pops. The whole church is praying." He walked to her bed and squeezed Macey's hand. Staring at her, he wondered why. He bent over and gently kissed her forehead, then leaned in and said, "Come back to me, Macey, please come back. I love you. I don't know what

I'll do without you. I'm not whole unless you are with me." He gave Pops a hug and said, "Sorry, but I can't stay. I've got another situation here in the ER I have to look in on. I'll be by later."

Chapter 18

Where, O death, is your victory?
Where, O death, is your sting?
1 Corinthians 15:55 (NIV)

It was a beautiful spring day, pansies and peonies in full bloom. Moms with strollers were out enjoying the unusually cool air, but Angus couldn't bring himself to appreciate the day. He felt a blackness, a dullness patiently waiting at the edge of his soul.

He locked the Bronco, trudged up the steps to the police station and dragged his feet to his desk.

"Angus, it's been five days," Jean said. "You need to take a rest. If anything happens to one of the girls, someone from the hospital will call."

He shuffled over to the coffee station and poured a cup. "I know, Jean, I know," he said chewing on a coffee stirrer. "I'm so tired. My days are spent here and my nights at the hospital. I have to be there when Macey wakes up. I have to know why. Why? If she *even* wakes up." His shoulders slumped. "Hey, Mark, thanks for working on the truck. I really appreciate it. I owe you."

"No problem. Glad I could help. You got enough on your plate."

Mark and Jean flashed each other a concerned look as Angus walked to his desk, pulled up the old library chair, and sat staring out the front window.

"Good to see people enjoying the day. God knows I can't, not even if I do take a vacation day. May as well be here doing something useful." He stood for a moment, placed his head against the cool window-pane, and fumbled with the ring box in his pocket. *Why didn't I tell her how I felt? Why did I wait? My heart hurts without her.* He sighed and resolved to tell her his feelings the first chance he got, no more Mr. Bravado.

He suffered a brief spat of cell shock when his new phone rang.

"Hello. I'll be right there," he said in a low and sullen tone.

"Jean, Mark, it's the hospital. Belissa is coming to. I'm going to see if I can get a statement and check on Macey while I'm there. I'll call you as soon as I have something." Angus grabbed his hat, took the steps two at a time and raced to the squad car.

He slipped quietly into Belissa's ICU room. Betty, her mom, was at her side stroking Belissa's hand and wiping away the little wisps of hair poking through the bandages on her head.

Belissa stirred. "Daddy, is that you?" she asked in a raspy voice as Angus entered the room. "Oh, Daddy, you finally came."

Surprised and uncomfortable, Angus stood at the bedrail. He looked at Belissa's mom, confused, unsure of what to do.

She nodded her head, mouthed the word please, and begged Angus with her eyes to play along.

Clearing his throat, Angus said, "I'm here, baby girl." Belissa squinted through her black eyes at him. He hated doing it, but had to ask, "Baby girl, what happened? Who did this to you?"

Barely above a whisper, Belissa turned and said, "It doesn't matter, Daddy. You came."

"Baby girl, who did this?"

"It doesn't matter, you're here."

"Baby girl, I need to know, please tell me."

"Lucas," she croaked. Belissa turned. "Mom, Mom, they're hurting me."

"Who, baby?"

"The monsters crawling on the wall. Fangs, Momma, teeth, Momma. The claws, it hurts. I am so tired, Momma. Please help me. They are laughing, and digging at me." Her eyes widened with terror, and her body twitched as she tried to escape the demons' claws.

"It's okay, baby girl. Jesus, Jesus, only you can help, sweet Jesus," her mom whispered.

"Again, Momma," as she tried to avoid her tormentors.

"Jesus."

"Again, Momma."

"Jesus."

"Better, Momma. I love you," she said as she rested her head back on the pillow.

"Momma?"

"Yes, baby," her mom answered as she wiped Belissa's brow.

Belissa winced in pain as she turned her head. "Daddy, I'm sorry. Love me?"

Angus cleared his throat again. "Yes, baby girl."

Belissa smiled. "Momma, tell Macey I'm sorry."

"Shh, not now, sweetie. You need to rest now. Don't talk."

"Momma, tell Macey I'm sorry for the note."

Angus drew back his hand in shock when he realized it was Belissa who wrote the note years ago, saying Macey wasn't pregnant.

"Daddy, Daddy, where are you?" Her chin trembled. "Don't leave me, not again. Come back, Daddy. Please, please."

Betty's tear-streaked face implored Angus to take her hand again.

She felt for his hand. "Oh, Daddy, you came back. Love me? I missed you so much."

Angus took a moment then mumbled, "Love you too."

"Momma, I've been so mean. Please forgive me."

"Baby girl, I love you. Please don't talk now. Rest, baby, just rest."

Belissa shivered, in terror she cried and groaned. "Say it, Momma. Say his name."

"Jesus, Jesus."

"Again."

"Jesus."

"Better, Momma. Momma?"

"Yes, baby."

"Momma, I see Jesus. Will he want to forgive me?"

"Oh, yes, baby. I know it."

Belissa squeezed both their hands. "It's him, Momma, I see him. The demons are gone, Momma," she said faintly, struggling for breath.

"You see him?"

"Mm hmm." Belissa moaned through bluish lips as Betty caressed her daughter's clammy face.

"Jesus, forgive me?" Smiling she said, "He said yes. Momma, he said he loves me, me?"

"Oh, baby girl, he loves you, so very, very much."

"Jesus, forgive me. I love you."

"Momma, he is calling me. Momma...I love you. Daddy, I love—" She gasped one last breath, causing the room monitors to beep wildly.

Her room filled with nurses and doctors, each with a specific preassigned task. One nurse dropped the head of the bed, another checked for a carotid pulse, while another nurse wheeled in the crash cart. The doctor instructed the team and ripped open Belissa's hospital gown while a nurse squeezed the gel on the defibrillator.

Angus went to Belissa's mom and both stared in horror at the kaleidoscope of blue, green, and yellow bruises covering Belissa's chest. It stunned Angus to see the faint outline of a boot in the bruising.

"My baby, my baby." Her mom wept and her knees buckled. "Oh, I can't look. Jesus, help me. Oh, sweet Jesus."

"Clear." The doctor ordered before Belissa's body jolted from the electrical shock.

"Nothing," the nurse said.

"Give her more epinephrine, another 1 mg. Come on, Belissa. Come on, Belissa."

The doctor shocked her again; no change.

After ten minutes, the doctor turned and pronounced, "Time of death 9:47 a.m.," and placed the bedsheet over her body as the nursing team emptied the room of the emergency equipment.

"I am so sorry, Mrs. Baker. The beating she took, along with the chemo, her body simply couldn't take anymore," the doctor said.

"Chemo?"

"She didn't tell you? She was getting ready to start her second round. Stage two ovarian cancer."

"No, no. No!" Belissa's mom cried and collapsed in Angus' arms.

"Mrs. Baker." He felt crushed for her and tried to soothe her. "She found Jesus, Mrs. Baker. You'll see her on the other side," he said and realized he meant it.

"Did you see her smile, Mrs. Baker? She's with him now. She's out of her pain and misery."

"I know, Angus. I so wanted to hug her one more time. Thank you for being there with me. At least now if I have any doubts, I have a witness. She found him, Angus, after all these years of praying, she met Jesus."

He spotted his mom walking toward Macey's room. Anne turned when she spotted Betty crying and rushed over while Angus helped Betty as she crumbled into the lobby chair. Bearing the pain of Betty's burden with her, his mom wept as she cradled Betty in her arms while gently comforting her with God's Word.

Angus was in turmoil. He hurried down the corridor to the hospital chapel. The smile and peace that came across Belissa's face moments before her death haunted him. Something miraculous happened. He peeked into the chapel. "Good, no one is here."

He walked to the front, dropped to his knees, and prayed earnestly. He asked God to forgive him of his pride, rejection and denial of him. With a deep sigh, he rested his head in his hands and wept over the sins he so willfully and habitually committed.

"God, I saw Belissa's face when she looked at you. You *are* real. Forgive me for ignoring you for so many years, pretending the things I did didn't matter. Forgive me for my anger, my bitterness, and my cruel tongue. I knew better, but I did what I wanted. Please forgive me. I need your peace."

Angus continued to pray as his shoulders quaked with repressed sobs. Regretful for the time he lost, he confessed his callousness and indifference towards Belissa and wept for her. Looking up at the cross he mouthed, "Thank you, God."

Grateful that God in his mercy gave both of them one more chance and each had accepted. Lamentations 3:23 came to his mind—"God's kindness and tender-hearted mercies are new every morning." *Odd that after years of neglect I can remember Scripture.* Angus was so thankful that he didn't bargain with God for Macey. He knew that whatever happened to Macey, with God, he could deal with it.

Deep in prayer Angus didn't notice his dad slip in next to him.

"Yes, they are, son. His mercies are new every morning."

Will talked with his son, his new brother in Christ, for over an hour discussing Belissa, Jesus, and the marvelous gift of salvation.

***

The line of cars for the funeral was comprised of the hearse, the limo with Betty, Angus' family in their suburban, and the pastor's car. One or two cars from Joey's followed the funeral procession.

At the cemetery, the birds were chirping; the grass was soft and giving, supporting them with each step taken. Butterflies hovered over the funeral sprays. Looking at the bouquets, Angus said, "Hey, sis, remember how you and Belissa chased the butterflies and how surprised she was to learn that ugly caterpillars turned into butterflies?"

"Pretty fitting. She has a new life now," Clara said wiping away a tear.

Angus looked at the sky and the small crowd near the gravesite. A few ladies from the church arrived along with Grammie and Willard. The crew from Joey's stood back, giving the family space to mourn and listened as Pastor Bill gave a moving and brief message on God's goodness. Slowly, the small crowd thinned as they tossed flowers on the casket. Angus watched as his mom walked with Betty to an ornate iron bench under a magnificent magnolia tree near the burial site. He cocked his head and listened in on their conversation.

"Oh, Anne, I so wanted to talk with her about Jesus to see her finally at peace, to brag of how God delivered her from witchcraft," Betty said blowing her nose.

"But you can Betty. He did deliver her. He answered each of our prayers." Looking at the sky, Anne continued, "I will always remember her as a little girl, laughing, always laughing. How she and Clara painted the dogs' toenails, the two of them dancing, twirling around the living room in their favorite thrift store evening gowns pretending to be princesses. Belissa was such a sweet girl, always smiling. I believe she's now looking down and smiling at you." Hugging Betty and looking at the clouds Anne said, "I am sure Jesus has told her of your earnest prayers for her, and I'm certain she'll thank you when you get to heaven. Then you can talk to her about the love and goodness of God."

***

Angus and Sherman drove through town looking for evidence of Lucas or anyone who might know his whereabouts.

"Geez, I wish I'd listened to Belissa's call earlier. She might still be alive if I did."

"No use in reliving that, Angus. What's done is done. You can't bring her back."

"I know, but still, I feel awful. At least she is in a better place now."

"You believe that?"

"Yes, I do. I haven't always lived the way a Christian should, with God's help I'll change."

"Hmm, wish I could believe. I've seen so much evil. Not sure if I have any faith left."

"I understand, but you need to realize that people have free will. God lets them choose what they can do, and when we sin or do wrong things, whatever you want to call it, it affects those around us. I take comfort in knowing that the Hitlers, serial killers, and others who have done horrible things, won't get away with what they have done. They may prosper for a while here on earth, but one day they'll answer to God and face his wrath. He's the final judge, and nobody at the end of the day or life gets away with anything evil if they haven't asked for forgiveness," he said.

***

"Hey, Angus is that Kathy?" Angus slowed the car to a stop pulling up next to her.

Sherman leaned out the window, motioning with her hand. "Kathy, you got a minute?"

"Sure, I guess. I'm on my way to work."

Angus twisted around in his seat to see Kathy. "Have you seen Lucas? Any idea where he is?"

"Nope." She crossed her arms, rolled her eyes and swallowed hard. "Haven't seen him." She picked up her pace walking toward the pharmacy.

"Okay, call us if you hear anything," Sherman said.

"Yah, sure. Gotta go."

"You see her expression change when you mentioned Lucas? She's lying."

Angus put the car in gear. "She knows something. She'll be in trouble if she is hiding him. Let's keep driving by her place. Maybe Rex will give Mark some extra hours to surveil her house and cruise by there during the night."

"Good idea," she said as they drove off toward the station.

Once inside the station, Angus grabbed another cup of coffee.

Jean looked up from her magazine and drummed her nails on the desk. "Angus, please stop pacing. You're making me nervous. The hospital will call if there are any changes with Macey."

"I know," he said sipping his hot drink.

"That ring is going to burn a hole in your pocket. You really should leave it at home. You don't want to misplace or lose her beautiful ring."

"I can't. I gotta have it with me when she wakes up." Angus winced when he burned his mouth on a big gulp of hot coffee.

Jean's cell phone rang.

"Hold that thought, Angus. I need to take this. It's my niece, she rarely calls. I hope everything is okay."

Chapter 19

Consequently, whoever rebels against the authority is rebelling against what God has instituted, and those who do so will bring judgment on themselves. Romans 13:2 (NIV)

"Becca, hold on a sec, I can barely hear you. I'm gonna put you on the speaker phone. What's going on?"

"I can't talk loud." Becca's voice trembled as she cupped her phone. Her voice faded for a moment. "I dropped my phone. Aunt Jean can you hear me? Someone is breaking into my dad's place."

Angus and Sherman leaned into the speaker phone.

"I came by on my way to work to check on Daddy. Remember, he had both knees replaced?"

"Yes, I saw him yesterday."

"His doctor released him last night."

Becca continued to whisper. "I came by to make sure he ate and well, anyway, I'm in the basement. I was starting laundry for him when I heard some guys break into the house." She put her hand over the phone. "They are upstairs walking around. Auntie, what do I do?"

A look of concern swept over Angus' face and his brow furrowed.

"Listen, honey, I will send Angus and Sher over ASAP."

Mark walked in and both Angus and Sherman put their fingers to their lips motioning him to be quiet. Puzzled, he mouthed, "Who's on the phone?" Perturbed, Sherman reached for a pencil and scribbled "break-in Jean's brother place" on a scrap piece of paper.

"Are you hiding?"

Becca crouched in fear. It took a moment before she could utter, "Shh, Auntie, they are opening the basement door."

The door creaked open and voices could be heard. Frustrated, Lucas hissed, "What are you doing?"

"I'm going to the basement. Old folks always have cool stuff down there. Might be something I can resell."

"No, you don't, you idiot." Lucas smacked him on the back of his head, grabbed him by the collar, looked at him, and said in a menacing tone, "You almost got us caught trying to sell old lady Weber's gold necklace." Then holding his fingers to his lips, he said, "Shut the door quietly."

Chokker wiped Lucas' spittle from his face and complied.

"Auntie, they aren't coming down. What am I gonna do?"

"You stay put, darling, and hide under the steps. Silence your ring tone and notifications, and don't come out until a deputy says so."

While Becca talked, Angus and Sherman gathered up their phones as Jean frantically wrote her brother's address down and handed it to Angus. She whispered, "I think it's Lucas. I thought I heard the name Chokker."

"Yah, I heard it too. That's his dumb as dirt pot smoking brother's nickname," Sherman said reaching for the squad car keys. "Let's go, Angus."

"Hey, you two got your vests on?" Jean asked and then turned back to calming her niece.

"Sure do," Angus said racing out the door. "Let's do a 10-40."

"Yah, a silent run is a good idea. We don't want to give him notice we are coming."

Sherman drove, taking the corners at high speed.

"Lucas has some nerve. It's five o'clock broad daylight. He's getting overconfident or low on money. I wouldn't be surprised if he's the one selling the prescription drugs around here," Angus said.

Sherman slowed the car down, parking at a house two down from Jean's brother's place. "10-23 arrived at scene." They both got out, quietly shutting the doors and grabbing their side arms at the same time.

With his hands, Angus motioned for Sherman to take the back door.

Angus crept up the front porch steps and avoided detection by stepping around the broken glass. *Idiots came through the front door.* He saw the perps' shadows on the wall. He reached in and slowly opened the front door.

"Listen, Chokker, get the drugs, and let's get outta here," Lucas said waving the revolver in the air.

"Hey, I thought we weren't gonna use guns? Dude, I ain't down with that."

"Shut up, you idiot. You'll wake him. 'Sides this is for protection, now let's go."

Upon entering, Angus hid behind a bookcase and saw Chokker walk across to Jean's brother's recliner.

Angus crept closer. *Stay asleep, Gary, stay asleep.* Heavily sedated, the old man continued snoring at jet engine levels.

Chokker snickered in his ear, "Nighty night old fart. Get some sleep while you can, tomorrow you will be in agony." He deftly picked up the bottle of pain pills from the pile of dishes and remotes.

As Chokker tucked the drugs in his pocket, he turned and saw Angus. His gun at Chokker's chest, Angus gritted his teeth and threatened, "Stop right there, or I'll shoot."

Chokker tried to run past him, but Angus tackled him and they crashed into a bookcase. Angus grabbed him and slammed him against the wall.

Lucas heard the crash. "Well, holy—!" shouting out expletives as he ran out the back door.

"You moron. Breaking and entering in broad daylight? You just broke into Jean's brother's house," Angus said.

"Jean who?"

"Uh, Jean, the sheriff's secretary."

Chokker groaned and slumped against the wall. Angus cuffed him and led him outside. He left the house as Gary continued snoring in his tattered recliner that creaked beneath his weight. Angus read Chokker his rights, put him in the squad car, and radioed Jean, "10-26, detaining one suspect and in pursuit of another."

He met Sherman at the side of the house.

"Why'd you stop chasing him?"

Sherman pointed in the direction of the six-foot chain link fence surrounded by thorny bushes and said, "No way over."

"Looks like our brilliant criminal mastermind just ran into the backyard of one of Macey's clients," Angus said as the sound of snarling, barking and growling flew through air. "I dropped her off here once. That house is what Macey calls the devil dog from hell home. She comes here to trim the nails and bathe the beast while the owner tackles and restrains the muzzled dog. It's a rescue. Don't go back there, not yet. When devil dog stops, we can go. Besides, Lucas isn't going anywhere." Angus gestured towards the fence to the far side of the backyard.

Lucas held the gun in his trembling hands. "Shut up! Shut up, you damn mutt!"

Gun at the ready, Angus watched the porch door creak open. The dog's owner stuck his head out. "What's going on back there? Lucifer? Where are you?"

"Shut up, or I'll shoot you," Lucas screamed as Lucifer, pulled and strained on the end of the chain cornering Lucas against the fence and the thorny rose bushes. Breathless, his heart pounding, he looked around searching for a way to escape.

Angus went ahead of Sherman, inching into the backyard with his gun drawn.

Lucifer, muscles taunt, lunged against his chain and lowered his head, growling at Lucas.

"Sir, get back inside," Sherman commanded the owner as she and Angus walked closer.

The homeowner yanked the dog's chain and yelled at his wife, "Mildred put that lousy phone down and get me the muzzle."

She paused her cell phone recording of the entire scene to get the muzzle. The screen door banged shut. "Lucifer, it's all right," the owner said as he struggled to place the restraint around the dog's frothy mouth. "Sorry, officer, he's a junkyard rescue. He can be vicious."

"I said go back inside and stay there. Leave the dog alone." Sherman said.

Angus went ahead of Sherman as they inched farther into the backyard, guns at the ready. While Sherman had her gun trained on Lucas, Angus yelled, "Drop your weapon! On the ground now! I said now!"

His chest tightened and the hair on his arms tingled. He knew something was going to happen. In a second, Lucifer broke free from his chain, and charged Sherman. She sidestepped, avoiding the crazed dog. Lucifer, fangs showing, jumped at her and she fired her weapon, grazing the dog. "Damn," she yelled.

Mildred screamed, "No!"

Lucas pushed his back into the fence, in an effort to avoid the dog.

"Put the gun down. I said put it down or I'll shoot," Angus yelled.

Lucas pretended to lower the gun to his side. He saw his chance and fired a shot, hitting Angus in the thigh; he went down with a groan as Sherman returned fire on a fleeing Lucas.

***

"Officer down! Officer down!" Sherman screamed into her shoulder com. "Lucas shot Angus. He's wearing jeans, white T-shirt, armed and dangerous. Last seen running north on Avenue A. Send an ambulance now to 509 Avenue A. In the back, hurry!"

Blood spurted from Angus' femoral artery as she yanked off her belt to use as a tourniquet.

"Come on, Angus, hang on. Don't you dare die on me." His eyes rolled back and his eyelids fluttered. "Hang on, the ambulance is almost here."

Tires screeched in front of the house.

"Jean," Sherman heard Mark on her com as he radioed in. "I am in pursuit of Lucas. Shots fired. Send Rex, send back up!"

***

Lucas ran, then turned and fired at Mark. Mark returned fire, hitting Lucas, sending him to the pavement. Lucas stared down at his chest as his blood gurgled out. He touched his chest, eyes wide in disbelief. "You shot me. You filthy—" He unleashed a string of racial slurs. "Argh," he groaned as he attempted to sit, causing more blood to bubble out. For a moment he stared at his bloodied hand and struggled to breathe, his lungs filling with blood.

Mark stood over him. "Lucas Lutz, you are under arrest for the murder of Belissa Baker, breaking and entering, and the attempted murder of a police officer."

Shocked, Lucas looked at Mark, he took one last raspy breath and died on the sidewalk. He felt the sensation of being in a vacuum. He touched his body. *Hole in the chest still there, check. I can think, check. I can see, check. But I'm alive? How is this possible?*

His body began to spin into a vortex of blackness and he smiled. *Well, if this is hell, it ain't so bad. I think I can handle this.* Lucas didn't know it, but he smiled his last smile for an eternity.

A cold, damp gray mist of pressurized darkness surrounded him, smothering him, as it slid up his legs, constricting his lungs, causing him to gasp for fresh air. There was none to be had. A deep despair wrapped around his mind like a blanket, refusing to let go, taking him to frightening places of abandonment and strangulating fear.

His endless life of horror began. The walls moved as a wave of putrid moisture came alive. Demons with scales, broken feathers, contorted broken arms, wings and legs at odd angles came crawling out of the wall and scurried over to him.

Slithering, the demons laughed at his ignorance, fetid and rancid drool escaping their jagged teeth. The stench of death penetrated his skin as the demons crawled on him, tearing at his skin and heart, eating his flesh. The painful sensation of being shot again and again tore through his *new* body.

He pressed his ragged body against the wall trying to escape, and let out a primal wail in agony. "I'm dead, I'm dead. There is no such thing as Hell! I'm sorry, God, I'm sorry." He raised his fist in anger. "Hey, hey! Where are you, God? I thought you were a loving God, why am I here?"

His burning eyes were seared, cracked, and dry, and with no moisture, he couldn't blink. Forever doomed to view the torment of others. Through his pain he saw emaciated silhouettes in the distance. He put his hands to his ears to drown out their screeches and moans. Their lifeless shadows walked slump shouldered, forcibly marched through the ocean of fiery sulfuric rain by demons. As they walked, the parched ground turned to burning embers searing their skeletal feet in pain. Lucas cowered, not able to understand how the barren land burned without vegetation to fuel the fire.

He heard a familiar voice. "Son, is that you?" Startled he felt a feeble bony, searing hot hand reach out to him in the darkness.

"Dad? Dad? Is that you?"

"It's me, son, it's me. It's no use. They got you too." Then his father's hand turned into a scaly, blood-dripping claw as a demon squealed with delight at his trick. The other demons laughed as they continued to tear at his chest.

He tried to run, but the burning flames of sulfur and lava engulfed his body as the demons congratulated each other on the lies Lucas believed.

Like a surreal film, Lucas' mind played scenes from his life. His words burned into his psyche, "Hey man, see you in hell!" followed by everyone's laughter. Drunk, and deep in discussion with his father, he remembered saying, "I'd rather be in hell where I can party instead of boring heaven surrounded by hypocrites." His words stabbed his soul, and a canyon of regret filled him, especially when he recalled the words he always said in anger, "Oh, go to hell."

"This can't be true. This can't be happening!" Lucas screamed as the demons tossed him like a rag doll between them. *I should've listened to Mom, and stayed in church.*

"Truth? He wants truth. I'll give you truth. This is your truth now." A heinous demon leered at him, picked him up, threw him against the mucus covered wall, and screeched, "The wages of sin is death."

All his life Lucas wanted nothing to do with God. Though God relentlessly pursued him, Lucas continued to deny God and his existence. He was in hell, a place where nothing good exists. No grass, sun, or water, not even a drop to quench his thirst. Death and decay surrounded him. He knew he'd never see sunshine again. His parched tongue clung to the roof of his mouth. He longed for cold water to refresh him. Lucas screamed, "No, no, no!"

He fell to the floor, overcome with grief, despair, and regrets. He knew he had begun his tour of hell forever.

***

"Angus, Angus." Crying, Sherman held him and said, "Stay with me. Hang on. Jean, Jean, where is the ambulance? Hurry, Lucas shot Angus!" She screamed into her shoulder radio. She cradled his almost lifeless form in her arms. Tears streamed down her face, mingling with Angus' blood, creating splotches of burgundy stains on her shirt and pants. Looking up she cried, "Please, God, let him live."

"Uh," Angus groaned.

"Stop moving. You've been hit in the femoral artery."

"Dammit, Jean, where's the ambulance?"

In the distance, sirens blared. "Hey partner, the ambulance is almost here. Hold on, Angus, hold on," she said wiping her face, smearing blood.

"Stay with me Angus, don't you dare die on me. Don't close your eyes. Look at me." Sherman hollered, "We're in the back," as she tried in vain to control the bleeding.

***

One paramedic checked for a pulse, while another took Angus' blood pressure. "He's lost a vast amount of blood." The other paramedic said, "His eyes are dilated. Hey, keep talking to him," he said to Sherman. "It might help him hang on."

"Hmm, this is weird," Angus said. He touched his legs and chest to see if he was standing next to Sherman. It occurred to him as he looked down why she was crying. His lifeless body lay on the ground as the paramedics worked frantically on the tourniquet.

Angus looked up, spinning at amazing speed away from the earth as it grew smaller and smaller. He passed clouds, then space, and finally heaven. He touched his leg. *Funny, there's no pain.* Bright luminous angelic beings with humanlike faces hovered around him. Each was immense in height and each held swords. Despite their size he felt no fear. They swished past him, flying, waiting above for him. Though their lips were still, he heard them talk with excitement. "He's ready. He's ready," they said with joy in their voices.

He looked at his legs. *Hey I'm floating!* He touched his arms, his belly, and face. *Is this for real? Are you angels?*

"Yes, Angus, we are here to help you as you transition to heaven." Though they didn't speak, he heard them.

Wait, you heard me? But I didn't say anything. How is that possible?

"All things are possible here, Angus."

He turned, and before him stood a magnificent set of gates made of one enormous pearl. At either side of the gates stood protecting angels. They held swords and shields and were dressed for battle. He remembered a verse from the Bible that said, nothing unclean shall enter here.

He wasn't sure how, but the ancient gates embodied righteousness and authority. Astounded, he marveled at the beauty surrounding him. As he passed through, the gates vibrated and spoke the words, "Behold the dwelling place of God Almighty."

Instantly he was transported to sprawling fields of flowers, vibrant in vivid yellows, and brilliant purples, blues, and reds. Every plant breathed and talked as they swayed in unison with the breeze over the field. There were rolling meadows, and trees with perfect fruit. Brilliant butterflies of all sizes fluttered past him. For a moment one landed on his hand and he felt its joy. Trees covered the valley, tall, majestic, moving, breathing. All creation cried out, "Glory to God. He alone is worthy to receive all praise."

Angus glided on, the emerald grass growing with each step. He was in awe of the surroundings, not a dead or dying leaf, everything, every last thing was bursting with life. Taking a deep breath, he filled his lungs with the purest sweetest smelling oxygen. In the few seconds since his arrival, his mind asked questions which were answered...by him! His new spirit comprehended his new home, his knowledge increased exponentially.

Angus remembered verses he had memorized from the book of Revelation. Christ's glory illuminated all things, there was no need for the sun. In the distance he saw the city of the living God. Its walls of variegated blue jasper stone radiated God's Glory. A river of transparent gold coursed through the streets to bring healing to the nations, to the people.

Angus gasped at the beauty and the diversity of the people. The perfection of his surroundings was almost unbearable. He looked ahead. A small child ran up to him. When the child touched him, Angus knew the child was his and Macey's. "Oh, Daddy, you made it!" the boy said giggling, tugging on his father's healed leg. Joyous, he reached down, spun his son in the air. Sheer bliss filled Angus as his son led him to a valley.

Overcome, Angus stood in awe at the splendor of the panoramic view. He looked ahead. "Wait, it can't be." Though he never met him, he recognized his Grandpa waving and calling to him.

Angus ran to him but stopped when he saw Him. Jesus, the world's Savior, powerful, mighty, and full of the wisdom of the ages stood before him. Angus raced to his Savior, and wrapped his arms around Jesus. He laughed and gave him a bear hug, and to his surprise, Christ hugged him, lifting Angus off his feet. Angus gazed into His eyes and knew he deserved death, but the grace, love, and forgiveness flowing through the eyes of Christ engulfed him. In adoration, Angus fell at his Savior's feet, overcome with joy. Peace and complete contentment pulsed in his heart.

Jesus' body marred by the cross reminded Angus of all he did for him. Trying to stand, his knees gave way, he fell at Christ's feet. Gently, Jesus lifted Angus. Elated, Angus flung his arms wide. "Because of your sacrifice I am here. It's true. Now is the day of salvation. All praise be to you, my Lord and Savior!" Christ smiled at the joy Angus displayed running about hugging other saints.

He called to him, "My son, my son, because you were my disciple on earth you are here with me now." At the sound of his voice Angus crumbled at his feet. King of Kings and Lord of Lords was written on his thigh.

Jesus paused, and lifting him again said, "Your time on earth is not done."

Angus clung to him, begging, "No, please don't send me back, I want to stay here, with you."

"I have many things for you to accomplish on earth in my name. You must go back." With alarming speed Angus raced through time and space, back to earth.

***

He stared down at the earth. At first it was a pinpoint, but as his speed increased it became larger and larger. His spirit raced through the atmosphere. With tremendous force he pierced the ambulance and was shoved into his bloodied body. The shock of the defibrillator filled him, as the pain pulsated through his body.

"We got an officer down," the paramedic yelled as they wheeled Angus through the glass ER doors. The hospital had gotten the call, nurses and doctors rushed about like a swarm of bees.

He saw Sherman crying, wiping his blood on her pants as she leaned against the wall for balance and support.

The nurses and doctors assessed the damage. He heard someone say, "Breathing is labored, and he's sweating profusely. BP is low, 65 over 40. The bullet severed his femoral artery."

Blood puddles had formed around the indentations of Angus' body on the gurney. He lay there watching the walls spin past him as he was wheeled into an ER bay. Blood was splashed on him and the paramedic like grotesque urban graffiti with his body as the canvas. The doctor ordered the trauma team nurse to cut his uniform.

"Prep for surgery here, now. We can't wait for a vascular surgeon. God help me. I have to do a femorosub-scrotal vein graft." He then added, "Nurse, see if you can get Dr. Kraft at the university on the line for me. Tell him it's an emergency. I'll have questions for him."

Angus saw his mom and others run down the hall towards him. *Mom, don't worry. I saw Jesus. I saw Him. Mom, can't you hear me?* He forgot that back on earth no one could hear his thoughts.

"Jesus, no, don't take him now. Please, no. What happened? My baby, my baby, what happened?" His mom wailed as Rex gently took her by the arm and led her away to the waiting room.

Again, more piercing pain, as the defibrillator delivered a searing shock to his heart, and Angus gasped a breath. For over an hour the trauma team continued to work.

***

Anne, Will, Clara, and Sherman looked up as the doctor came toward them. Removing the surgical mask, he said, "Are you the family?"

"Yes. I am Mrs. Connors, his mother."

"Well, Mrs. Connors, I think he will make it. I was able to stop the bleeding. We're taking him up to get a CAT scan to make sure there is no additional damage to his veins. He is a very fortunate man. He died once on the way over, and once here we had to shock him again, but I believe the worst is over."

"Oh, thank you, Lord," she said, "Can I see him?"

"Yes, but only for a few moments."

***

By the time Mark's squad car reached the station, a crowd had gathered. Lucifer's owners had quickly posted the arrest video to their social media, and the local Gazette editor was already there taking a few in-your-face pictures of Larry in handcuffs for the morning paper. He jotted down on his notepad the headline Crime Spree Ends!

"Officer Foreman, how do you feel about this arrest? Is he the one who has been breaking into homes?" the editor asked.

"No comment," Mark replied.

"Chokker, I mean," the editor said shaking his head remembering the perps real name, "Larry Lutz, any comments?"

"Yah, police brutality. I didn't do nothing," he said spitting on the cement as Mark led him up the steps to the police station jail cell.

Mark removed the cuffs, opened the door, and tossed Chokker in. With a bang he slammed the cell shut rattling the windows and the door at the station.

"Hey, where's Lucas? Hey! Hey, tell me where's Lucas. Where's my brother?"

"He's dead," Mark said.

"Dead? What?" In an instant Chokker's mind went from concern about his brother to self-preservation.

"Hey, listen, I gotta tell you something," Chokker hollered and pressed his face to the cell bars. "I ain't taking the heat by myself. Hey, Mark, hey, Jean, you wanna know who the mastermind is behind the drugs and break-ins?"

"Well, it sure isn't you, Larry, you're too dumb. If brains were leather, you wouldn't have enough to saddle a Junebug."

He rolled his eyes at Jean and said, "Listen, before I say anything, I want a lawyer, and a Payday candy bar," Larry demanded.

"What?" she asked.

"You heard me, a lawyer and a Payday candy bar. I'm hungry, and I'm bettin this information will be like a payday to y'all."

Irritated, Mark got up, walked over, unlocked the cell, and cuffed Larry.

"Hey, police brutality. That hurts. Are cuffs really necessary? Come on, it's me, Mark. Ya know Chokker?"

"Yes, it's necessary," Rex said as he strode in the door laying his cowboy hat on Jean's immaculate desk, covering her Hollywood gossip magazine. Moments later, a disheveled Sherman came in.

"I am afraid to ask, but how is Angus?" Jean asked as Mark listened to the conversation.

"The doctor says he'll make it. It's a true miracle. He died twice, but he's going to be around a lot longer. Doctor thinks he'll be back to work anywhere from two to six weeks tops."

"What's that you were saying, Chokker?" a perturbed Rex asked walking towards his office.

"I can tell you what you want to know 'bout everything," Chokker replied.

"All right, what ya got?" Mark asked. He walked Chokker to Rex's office and shoved him into a metal chair. He shut the door, and sat at the table across from him, next to Sherman.

"Easy, Mark, I don't want anything to go wrong. Not a scent of police brutality. I've been after these two greasy yahoos for a while," Rex said pulling up a battered wooden chair next to Larry.

Before Rex could continue, a knock interrupted them.

"What now?" Rex bellowed.

The office door squeaked open, its bottom scraping against the wood floor as a portly man dressed in pressed jeans stepped in. "Not another word with my client." Chokker tried to speak but was cut off. "Let me handle this, Larry."

"Might have known it'd be you Bulldog," Rex said as the man left muddy boot prints on the floor.

"Good to see you too Rex."

Mark knew years of contempt had accumulated between Rex and Bulldog. Bulldog's shady lawyering and getting criminals off on technicalities angered his boss.

Rex kicked a chair towards him, hitting Bulldog in the shins.

"Apology accepted."

"None given." He shoved the charges across the desk.

Snatching the papers with his yellowed nicotine-stained fingers, Bulldog said, "Certainly, these charges are trumped up."

"Yah, that's right."

"Chokker, I mean Larry, please be quiet."

"Well I got a lot to say, I'm not going down all by myself. I want a deal."

"Shut up, Larry."

Rex stretched, put his feet on his desk and smiled at Bulldog as Larry kept talking. An hour later, Larry and his lawyer, along with Mark, Sherman, and Rex, came out of the office.

"We need to make a few more arrests. Don't screw this up. Read Kathy her Miranda rights. Say nothing more than you have to, Mark. She won't put up a fight," Rex said and continued, "I'll get Kelvin. He's a sly one, and with him being the assistant to the mayor, he's bound to lawyer up if he hasn't already. Lord knows news travels fast in this town."

"I can't believe she hid him under her shed!" Sherman said shaking her head in wonder at what Chokker had disclosed to them. "She really dug a pit under her shed floor for him? Guess there is no telling what family will do for each other."

Chapter 20

If we are faithless,
he remains faithful,
for he cannot disown himself. 2 Timothy 2:13 (NIV)

"Angus, I wish you would stop your pacing," Jean said irritated.

"I can't. Not knowing is driving me crazy. Why did she jump?" he said, fingering the engagement ring in his pocket. Resignation set in, and he dragged himself over to the window. Leaning his arm against the cool glass, he wondered aloud, "How did this happen? I replay everything in my mind. I just can't figure it out."

He was startled from his thoughts when Jean's phone rang.

Angus checked his cell phone for the millionth time. He spun around. *Please be the hospital with good news.*

"That's the hospital. You need to get there ASAP."

He scooped up the car keys. Limping, he grabbed his cane and took the stairs as fast as he could.

With sirens blaring, he pulled into the hospital emergency parking lot.

"That was sure fast," his mom said. "Glad you got here right away. Less than ten minutes in what is usually a twenty-minute drive."

"Never mind that. How is she?"

"I think you had better see for yourself."

Angus rushed as fast as he could down the hall to room 110.

He paused and stood at the doorway, staring at the variety of colored wires and tubes coming from the bed leading to several monitors in the room. Nurses were taking vitals. Angus wasn't sure what to expect as the doctor rushed past him.

He watched and listened as the doctor leaned over the bed. "Okay, Macey, follow the light with your eyes," he said, passing the pencil light to the left, right, and up and down.

"Good, good. Your vision appears to be fine. How many fingers am I holding up?"

"Three."

"Good. What is your name?"

"Macey Wilson."

"Can you tell me who this is standing next to you?"

"That's my grandpa, Pops." With a big smile Pops squeezed her hand.

"Okay, it looks like all is good, but we'll run another CT scan to confirm there is no damage or any other swelling. But for now, I would like to officially say, Macey Wilson, you are a miracle." Before leaving to check on another patient, he gave the nurse additional instructions.

Angus looked intently at Macey and hadn't noticed Pastor Bill or the others next to her bed. He stood silent, frozen as a broad smile crept over his face. Macey was sitting up in bed, with Pops standing next to her holding her hand.

***

Pastor Bill said, "Pops has never left your room. He's been praying 24/7. What did you tell me earlier today?"

Pops kissed her hand, and said, "Macey, God showed me in a dream the great buffalo, eagle, and a cross. I knew then with a certainty you would not die." He smiled and looked up. "I prayed to God, our great warrior, to fight on your behalf, for your healing. God has been good."

"You have been covered in prayer. Praise God, what an answer he has given us," Pastor Bill said.

"How long has it been?"

"A little over a month," Pops replied.

"I never knew I was so loved," Macey said as she looked at the others in the room. Grammie, Willard, Clara, Bryan, Anne, and Will, along with the entire church pastoral team stood near her. Each hovered around the bed chattering with excitement.

"How do you feel?" Clara asked.

Bryan wanted to know what being a coma was like and Grammie asked, if she had a headache. The questions continued nonstop, each interrupting the other in their excitement.

Angus stepped in closer and cleared his throat loudly. An immediate parting of bodies cleared the way to Macey's bedside.

Macey looked up and noticed the concerned, yet anguished look on Angus' face.

"Let's give these two some alone time," Will said. Anne and Clara exchanged knowing looks as everyone left the room, hugging and laughing at the marvelous miracle God had performed.

***

Angus approached the bed slowly. "Hey, babe, I am so glad to see you. How ya feeling?" he asked as he leaned in to give her a kiss.

Macey turned away and buried her head in the pillow.

"Macey, I don't understand. Why are you upset with me? Why did you jump? You gotta know I love you. Why, Macey why?" he implored and took her hand in his.

Tears ran down her face, and he continued, "Every girl I've ever dated was only a poor likeness of you, a shadowy replica that never satisfied my heart. I kept telling myself I didn't need you, but I was so wrong." He reached to brush away a tear and she again, turned away.

"Please, Macey give me a second chance. I can't go on without you. Your beautiful face is the last thing I see at night when I close my eyes and escape to you. Yours is the first and only face I see in the morning as I stir from my dreams of you. You surround me, I can't go on without you. I refuse to. One more chance, Macey, that's all I ask, please. We can have a future, a future of hope, love and lifelong commitment. Tell me why? I don't understand. What did I do?"

"You know why," she said as she burst into tears.

"No, I don't."

"I went to take you your favorite blueberry pie for our picnic," she said between sniffles.

"Uh huh."

"Well, when I got to your place, Belissa was there." She cried louder, burying her head in the tiny hospital pillow.

His eyebrows scrunched together. "What are you talking about?"

"She was there, wearing your robe with nothing on underneath." Macey blew her nose between sobs. She came out of your bedroom, and said, 'Oh, Angus, stop that!' Her hair was all messed up. She looked at me standing there like an idiot. I dropped the pie on the kitchen floor and ran out."

Angus chuckled. "And here, I thought Grammie was nosing around my place and brought me a pie and dropped it and didn't bother to clean it up. No wonder she looked puzzled when I asked her about it.

"Look at me, Macey, honey, please believe me. It *did not* happen."

"Yes, it did," Macey wailed and turned her head away.

Looking at her intently, Angus smiled and held her head in his hands, "No, I tell you, it did not happen. I wouldn't lie to you. I got a ride into work. The starter went out on my truck. I had Sher pick me up. You can ask her. I was at work. I'm telling you I was at work."

"You were?" she asked.

"Yes, babe, I was. I would never get back with Belissa. Besides, you don't have to worry about her anymore."

"Why, what do you mean? She's always been trying to separate us."

"I know, but that can't happen ever again."

"Why?"

"She's dead, Macey," Angus said looking at the floor.

"What? When?" she asked covering her mouth with her hand.

"While you were jumping, she got the sh—, oops I'm sorry. I didn't mean to cuss. I meant that she was brutally beaten by Lucas. We took a call about a disturbance at Joey's BBQ, and when we got there, we found her barely alive, laying near her apartment door.

"I feel responsible. She tried calling me, but I ignored the call. She succumbed to the injuries, and we caught Lucas breaking into Jeans brother's house a few weeks ago. But he's dead too."

"Dead, Lucas?"

"Yah, he and Chokker, I mean Larry, have been breaking into houses taking prescriptions and selling them."

"What happened to your leg? Why are you on limping and using a cane?" Macey asked alarmed.

"Uh, Lucas shot me." Not wanting to worry her he said, "It's nothing really," adding in his best British accent, "It's just a flesh wound."

"Oh! You and your Monty Python! I can't believe he shot you. I'm so glad you are okay."

"No more questions for me. I need to ask you something."

Angus knelt by her bed, opened the ring box and said, "Macey Wilson, the one true love of my life, the one girl I could never forget about, will you do me the honor of being my wife?"

Macey gasped at the ring, hesitantly reached out her hand, and then pulled it back. She cried, and covered her face with her hands and said, "No."

Stunned, he shook his head and stepped back. "I don't understand. You don't have to worry about Belissa." Then a light went on in his head. "Oh, you're still struggling with what happened and me leaving you?"

"That's part of it. Can you forgive me?"

"Oh, babe, I forgave you the day I found out. Unforgiveness is an ugly thing. It's the one thing that stuck with me from being in church. Unforgiveness poisons the soul. I love you, Macey. So, you will marry me?"

"I'm sorry, Angus. I want to, but I can't," she said through her tears.

"You can't, why?" he asked, bewildered.

She hung her head, tears splashed onto her hands, "You don't love the Lord the way I do. We would be unequally yoked. I truly want to, but I can't marry you. We would end up unhappy and arguing about how to raise kids, going to church, all that stuff. You know I'm right."

Angus hung his head, took a deep breath, and said, "Yah, you are right. Macey, I accepted Christ the day Belissa died. Watching her die, I saw the comfort, peace, and joy that came over her face when she asked Jesus to forgive her. He's real, I've always known. I was just running from God, but I'm not anymore. It's real. Ask my dad. He found me in the chapel here, and we talked and prayed."

"Say it. I need you to say it. My heart needs to hear you say it."

"Macey, it's real, Jesus is my savior."

Macey sat up again and smoothed her gown. Giddy, she held out her hand, and giggled. "Ask me again, Angus."

He bent over her bed, and placing the ring on her finger, he said, "Macey Wilson, the one true love of my life, and the one girl I could never forget about, will you do me the honor of being my wife?"

"Yes, Yes! Angus, I will marry you," she squealed.

They kissed and heard a noise from the nurses' station. "Well, it looks like we have had an audience this whole time," Angus said.

Looking up, at the large picture window, they saw everyone's face pressed against the glass. The crowd burst into clapping and jumping when Macey said yes. Upon hearing the good news, Clara, Anne, and Tonya, who had just arrived, almost trampled one another as they rushed past Angus to Macey's bed, nearly knocking him over. Talking all at once about wedding plans, taking turns admiring her ring.

Clara said, "Brother, wow, you did great. That's one *be-u-tee-ful* ring!"

"Tonya, you had the babies! You must be so tired," Macey said.

"Yes, I am. They came early, but they are healthy. I had to see you," she said smiling.

"What are their names?"

"Well, they are kind of unusual. One is Manny, short for Manasseh, the middle boy is Mark, and our girl—"

"A girl! I thought the doctor said you were having boys?" Macey squealed.

"Yes, well, a girl snuck in there! We named her Myrrh."

"Oh, I love her name," Macey cooed.

"I can't stay long though. Kolby is with them, so I need to get back. Let me know the wedding plans, Clara, will you? Macey, stop by when you are released," Tonya said as she gave Macey a quick hug and headed for the door.

The nurse came in, and said "Someone's had an exciting day." She took her pulse. "Ladies, she looks tired, so I'll have to ask you all to leave."

"Okay, let's go. Macey, we'll be back tomorrow and talk some more about the wedding," Clara said.

"Okay, guess I'd better go too. I'll be back first thing in the morning. I love you," Angus said and kissed her goodbye.

"I love you too. Angus, the ring is simply gorgeous." She grinned and returned his kiss.

"Okay, you two lovebirds time for some rest," the nurse said gesturing for Angus to leave.

Chapter 21

That is why a man leaves his father and mother and is united to his wife, and they become one flesh. Genesis 2:24 (NIV)

"Who'd of thought that three months ago we'd be getting married?" Angus said, as he drove the Bronco through a quiet neighborhood, Macey at his side.

"Hey, I've got something to show you." Angus stopped, and pulled his Bronco to the curb, parked, and got out to stretch his leg.

"What? What could you possibly have to show me? We've been driving around running wedding errands for hours."

"I'm getting a cramp and need to walk." He walked over to open her door.

"Too many cake samples?" she commented as they walked down the street, stopping at a cul-de-sac.

"Isn't this the cutest little house? It's for sale. It'll be a while before we can get a house though. I'll be patient." She sighed and took his hand.

A woman in a black suit approached them. "It's not for sale anymore," the realtor said as she came up the walk and slapped a large red SOLD sticker across the front. Turning, she handed Angus the house keys saying, "Congratulations first-time homeowners."

"Tah dah!" he said. "It's ours. I signed the loan this past week."

"What! It's ours? Angus, I can't believe you did this." She gave him a big hug, grabbed his hand and dragged him up the steps.

"Would you look at this porch? It's beautiful, I can put a swing right there," she said as she pointed to the corner. "A wreath on the door would dress it up and I can hang flowers. Pops and I'll plant some peonies, daisies, and lilacs in the yard. You did remember Pops? You planned on him being here, right?"

"That old man, uh, yah, no, I don't think so. Newlyweds need a place of their own," Angus said.

He, grinned and smoothed his shirt, and then opened the front door to Pops standing in the small entryway.

"You remembered!"

"Of course, I did. Hey, crazy old man, did you pick your room yet?"

"Yes, I did. I'll take the back bedroom, that way I can admire the yard and have my coffee on the back porch."

Delighted, Macey clapped her hands and said, "It has two porches?"

"Yes, two porches. The back one is screened in. There's a large living room, a good-size kitchen that has a dishwasher, and breakfast nook. There's a powder room near the basement door, and the upstairs has two more bedrooms and one full bath. And, you'll love this, a huge fenced backyard."

"Fenced? Really?" Her eyes sparkled as she pulled him to the back door, not pausing to appreciate the hard-wood floors throughout or the ample kitchen storage and cabinets.

"Oh, honey, a fenced yard. So, we can get a dog or better yet, dogs? There's this dog, Tank's his name. You're going to love him. He's at the SPCA. Nobody wants him. Brenda, the shelter worker, gave me a call about him two weeks ago. He's a real gentle giant," Macey said in rapid fire fashion.

"Uh, I don't think so, at least not yet. Okay? Let's take it one step at a time. Last thing I want is a slobber beast in the house and the land bombs. Big dogs are a lot of work, Macey." He saw her look of disappointment, and heard her sigh. "I hope you understand. Come on, let's not talk about that now. Let's get some of Pops' stuff out of my car so he can unpack while I run one more errand. Want to come with me?"

"Um, I'm not sure. Maybe not, but the sly look on your face tells me you have something else to show me," she said as they held hands walking the fence line. Macey prattled on talking about paint colors as they surveyed the yard, and headed to the car.

Stopping at the front, Macey said, "It's gorgeous, no more teensy, rental living. We can put in a picket fence and a stone walkway, a porch swing and—"

"Hold off on the honey dos. Let's get married first," he said opening the car door for her.

"Okay," she said and slid over next to Angus. "Where are we going now?"

"You'll see, now cover your eyes, no peeking!" he said. To confuse her he drove slow taking extra turns.

Macey squirmed, giggled, and in her best southern drawl said, "I just love surprises. Why, Angus, whatever would I do without you?"

He parked the Bronco and warned her again, "Okay, no peeking. I mean it. I'll come around and help you out. Keep your eyes closed."

Still covering her eyes, Angus walked Macey up the sidewalk to the door. Inside he helped her sit on the leather bench as Brenda tiptoed over and unleashed Tank. His nails clicked against the tile floor as he raced to her.

"Okay, open your eyes."

"Tank! Tank! He's mine? Ours?" she said, hugging Tank tightly around his massive neck.

"Yes," Angus sighed. "I hope I don't regret this."

"Tank, my baby! Who told you?"

"Well, Clara mentioned you come here every day before and after work fawning over Tank. She said you've been visiting him for the last two weeks. I called her this morning, had her bring me the fancy pants, organic, expensive dog food that is collecting dust at the clinic, and then I had her pick up a collar and leash. I came by yesterday and adopted him. He's yours."

"I can't believe you did this." She squeezed Tank's jowls as he licked her face.

"Geez, Macey, how can you do that? Stinky dog breath. Am I supposed to kiss those lips after the dog has licked you?"

"Yup, you'll just have to get used to it."

"Thanks, Brenda, I think. We got to get back to the house," he waved goodbye as they walked out the shelter doors.

"Bye, Brenda," Macey said as she and Tank ran across the faux fire hydrant-lined sidewalk to the Bronco.

He opened the door, Tank leapt into the back seat and to Angus' surprise so did Macey. She gave Tank another hug and then promptly rolled down the window. They both stuck their heads out while Angus drove back to the house. Macey laughed, her hair flowing in the breeze as Tank's jowls and ears flopped in the wind.

***

"The big day is here." Macey's face beamed as Clara carefully arranged her hair and did her makeup.

"I know. Do you remember when we were kids, how you dreamed about marrying Angus and how I said it was gross?"

"Yes, I do. And now it is finally happening."

"It's such a gorgeous day, not a cloud on the horizon. I can smell the lilacs. The Botanical Garden is so pretty this time of year," Clara said as she looked from the window at the generously blooming gardens below. Cloth covered chairs were arranged on the luscious, verdant green lawn. At the end of each aisle, lavender peonies, roses, and ribbon sprays were attached.

The gazebo at the front was adorned with more lavender and pink roses, lilacs, and peonies. Clara hummed the bridal tune as she watched family and friends being seated.

Anne looked out the window and grasped her hands close to her in surprise. "I can't believe Pastor Tuttle came. He baptized you and your brother when you were toddlers." She clapped her hands, turned to Macey and said, "So do you have everything? Something old, something new, something borrowed, something blue?"

"Well, I have these beautiful bejeweled Converse wedding sneakers for something new," Macey said.

"Wow, those are gorgeous," Anne said as she admired the sequins and crystal-studded shoes that had white ribbon shoelaces and the word bride embroidered on the back. "Where did you find those?"

"These are from Tonya. Don't you just love them?" Macey said as she modeled the shoes for each of them.

"What about borrowed?" Anne asked.

"I have Grandma's earrings for her. See?" Clara said as she made a small adjustment to Macey's hair and put the pearl earrings in. "The salon did a fantastic job on your hair."

"I know," Macey said as she patted her hair in the mirror. "Can you see the crystal butterflies, flowers and feathers, and miniature silver arrowheads I had the beautician put in?"

"Yes," Anne said, "Your updo is simply stunning."

Overjoyed, Macey said, "I know. But we couldn't think of anything blue, so we decided we would each paint our nails baby blue. We got manicures yesterday. I don't have anything old."

"I have just the thing," Anne said as she walked over to a large hatbox and opened it, removing layers of white tissue paper. "Macey, I was cleaning out the cabin years ago, and I came across a box of toys. Your Ken and Skipper dolls were in the toy box. It took some scrubbing but I was able to get the dirt off of Skipper. Anyway, I remembered you telling me you would marry Angus one day, so I saved them. I hope you don't mind but I had a new bouquet made."

Anne lifted the flowers out of the box. Embedded in the white and lavender bouquet were Macey's Ken and Skipper dolls from long ago. Anne flipped the flowers over. "Their legs are the handles for the flowers. Look, you can still see the heart you drew on the Skippers face years ago."

"Oh, Anne, that's so thoughtful. I love, love, love it! Look it says Angus + Macey on Kens legs!" She hugged Anne, then showed Clara and Tonya the bouquet. "I'll walk down the aisle with these and throw the other bouquet. I'll keep my doll bouquet forever," Macey said admiring her dress in the mirror.

A knock at the door interrupted them and Pops whispered, "It's time, Macey girl."

"Okay, Pops. I am ready, and so is Tank."

***

A nervous Angus waited at the gazebo, fidgeting. He adjusted his deep blue cummerbund on his black tuxedo, and fiddled with his cufflinks and straightened his vest. Pastor Bill and Angus watched with anticipation waiting for the bride to appear. Escorting Tonya, Kolby walked in first wearing pale blue pants, matching vest and striped lavender shirt underneath, and a bow tie. Tonya wore a knee-length light blue off the shoulder dress, and held a small pastel bouquet in her hands. Bryan and Clara came next in the same attire.

Tank followed them down the aisle with a collar made of pastel flowers and sporting a black and blue large bow tie. A few paces behind Tank were the flower girl and ring bearer. The crowd stood as the traditional *Here Comes the Bride* music began.

Tank stopped short of the steps to the gazebo as Anne took him by his collar and sat him next to her.

With Macey on his arms, Pops stood tall, his shoulders back, beaming with pride and in his Native American leggings and leather beaded deerskin top.

With sweaty palms, Angus stood waiting for Macey. When he saw her, he grinned and fixed his attention on her.

Macey was striking in her knee-length wedding dress layered with taffeta and chiffon. The dress had a bodice of lace, pearls, crystals, and a sweetheart neckline. Radiant, she reached out to Angus and took his hand.

Pastor Bill opened his Bible and read from I Corinthians 13. "Love is patient, love is kind. It does not envy, it does not boast, it is not proud. Love is not rude, it is not self-seeking, it is not easily angered, and it keeps no record of wrongs. Love does not delight in evil but rejoices with the truth. It always protects, always trusts, always hopes, always perseveres. Love never fails. And now these three things remain: faith, hope, and love. But the greatest of these is love." He paused and motioned for the two of them to step closer.

"Angus, Macey remember love is an action, it is an act of your will. There will be times of joy and times of difficulties. During those times of difficulty show kindness toward the one you love. Be patient, do not seek your own interests. Be committed to each other, and don't hold grudges."

He continued, and once finished, asked Angus then Macey the traditional wedding questions.

"I do." Angus smiled at Macey and placed the ring on her slender finger.

Pastor Bill grinned and continued, "Macey, do you take Angus to be thy lawfully wedded husband?"

"Yes, I do!" she exclaimed placing the gold wedding band on Angus' finger.

"Ladies and gentlemen, I present to you, Mr. and Mrs. Angus Allen Connors. Angus, you may kiss your wife."

Angus gently bent her over his arm, giving her a loud, noisy, and long kiss.

After the bride and groom were introduced as husband and wife, Pops stepped forward and began the traditional Indian blanket ceremony.

"Angus and Macey, I now cover you each in these two blue blankets." Turning to the guests, he added, "The blue blankets I am placing over you symbolize your individuality. Your past life will no longer be. As our great God and Holy Spirit bless this union, I now unite and bless you."

He smiled and continued, "Treat yourselves and each other with respect and remind yourselves often of what brought you together. Give the highest priority to the tenderness, gentleness, and kindness your connection deserves. When frustration, difficulties, and fear assail your relationship, as they threaten all relationships, remember to focus on what is right between you, not only the part which seems wrong. In this way, you can ride out the storms when clouds hide the face of the sun in your lives—remembering even if you lose sight of the sun, it is still there. And if each of you takes responsibility for the quality of your life together, it will be marked by abundance and delight."

He paused and wiped a tear away and then removed the blue blankets. Macey and Angus stepped closer to each other.

"I now place this single white blanket over the two of you, symbolizing your future of peace and happiness.

May your love be like a running brook, clear strong and ever present. An eternally following stream that sings its melody to the night. May your heart wake with joy at dawn, giving thanks for another day of love. Promise each other to return home at each night with gratitude and a loving embrace. I pray that anger will vanish in the night. That you will sleep with a vision of the beloved in your heart and a song of tenderness in your dreams." Standing tall, his face beamed as he continued.

"Angus, may your fountain be blessed, and may you rejoice in the wife of your youth. Macey, may peace always be within your walls. And may you and your household always serve the Lord. May his favor shine on you as you seek after him. In Jesus' name."

And everyone said, "Amen."

Once the ceremonies were completed, and pictures taken, the guests were seated for dinner.

Kolby stood. "Ahem," he said and tapped his spoon against his champagne flute. "Family and friends, I'd like to give a toast." Raising his glass high, he motioned to Angus.

"This ought to be interesting," Angus whispered to Macey.

"We have been friends for a long time, since second grade when you rescued me from the school bullies. You were my anchor in middle school and all that happened then. You've been Robin to my Batman. Yes, you heard me correctly, I said Robin. You've helped me to invent things and encouraged me to be a science teacher." Kolby pulled a worn piece of ledger paper from his pocket and unfolded it. "Remember this invention?" he said holding the creased paper to the light, looking at the guests he added, "If you can't see this look under your plate there should be a copy."

Angus chuckled. "Oh, man. I can't believe you saved that."

"Dude, what else is a nerd supposed to do? We were certain kids all over the world would want the Mighty Mattress that had super bounce abilities." He held the drawing up, showing a stick Angus jumping off of the second story roof onto the stacked mattresses below.

Large red lines showed the figure bouncing at impact, then bouncing on to the trampoline, and lastly the pool. Angus shook his head and laughed. "As you can see, my calculations were sorely lacking. Thank God your mom came out to stop you right before you jumped."

The wedding guests laughed as Kolby turned to Macey. "You are getting the best guy here. My stunt man, my wingman, my best man. May God richly bless you in your new life together." He turned to Angus. "And dude may your quiver be full, but I honestly don't think you can beat triplets, ever."

Cheers and laughter filled the wedding hall. The bride and groom cut the three-tier cake that had an Indian Maiden and Policeman at the top.

While the guests enjoyed the wedding cake, the DJ announced the bride and groom dance. Angus stepped up to the platform and took the microphone from him and said, "Excuse me everyone I would like to say a few words to my lovely bride. Macey, I wrote this poem for you. I hope you like it." He took a notecard out of his breast pocket and began.

"I, who had nothing
Have my everything with you
I, who had felt nothing
Have my world awakened by you
I, who loved nothing
Have abandoned my heart you
I, who am nothing
Have worth because of you
I, who knew nothing
Have realized love in you

Macey, you alone possess my heart. Who am I that you should love me? I am blessed and honored to be your beloved." He lifted a glass to toast his new bride and said, "Macey Connors, I like the sound of that. I love you."

When he finished, he walked to her gently kissed her hands and guided her to the dance floor. "Come join me in our first dance as husband and wife." The DJ played the same wedding song his parents and sister danced to at their weddings, *Waltzing With My Darling,* by Jim Reeves.

Once the traditional dances were done, Macey stepped onto the floor for the throwing of the bouquet. All the hopeful single women gathered around, jockeying for a position to catch the flowers. Macey counted to three and threw the bouquet. Unfortunately for Sherman, no one had noticed Tank in the lineup. As she was about to grab the flowers, Tank jumped at the bouquet knocking her to the floor. Angus hurried after him and retrieved the almost demolished flowers before he could eat them.

"Oh, Sher, I am so sorry," Macey exclaimed.

"Are you all right?" Mark asked.

"Yes, my pride hurt is all." Embarrassed, Sherman stood, smoothed her dress, and ignored Mark, who had extended his hand to help her up.

Angus spotted his dad about to begin his 3rd dance in a row with Grammie and decided he needed rescuing. He walked over and said, "Hey, Dad can we take a walk?"

"Sure, son."

The two of them stepped outside the covered tent area.

"Dad, I gotta say I am nervous. How have you and Mom stay married for so long? I know from the stories you have told me and Clara that you and mom have been through a lot of tough times. You and Pastor Bill are the only people I know who haven't divorced or remarried."

"Well, son, it's definitely a God thing. You don't know the half of what we have been through. I guess I can say we went into marriage knowing no matter what divorce wasn't an option for us. We were determined on that.

"I could talk for days about what God has brought us through, but let's save that for another day, okay?"

"Um, sure. Hey, I think I hear the DJ asking people to get up and dance. We'd better go in."

"All the gentlemen please come to the dance floor. It is time for the Electric Slide with a side of wiggle! Not sure what that means, but they told me to introduce the dance that way," the DJ said laughing.

That night, after the dancing, the new couple stood arm in arm. Beaming with love, they thanked their friends and family who had prayed for and stood by them, content in finally being able to enjoy all of life's adventures and God's blessing that awaited them.

If you have enjoyed *Bridge to Redemption,* please share your thoughts with your family and friends. Reviews are the driving force of an author, as a writer I ask that you please take a moment to leave a review on Amazon. I am grateful and appreciate your support.

If you would like to learn more about the Connors family a prequel will be coming soon. Be sure to check out and like my Facebook Author's page, CeCe Writer.

CPSIA information can be obtained
at www.ICGtesting.com
Printed in the USA
LVHW040811050820
662303LV00002B/258